ASSAULT ON HELL

By Volk Presmaren

MARTIAN PUBLISHING

This is a work of fiction.
Any resemblance to persons or
organizations, living or extinct,
is entirely coincidental.

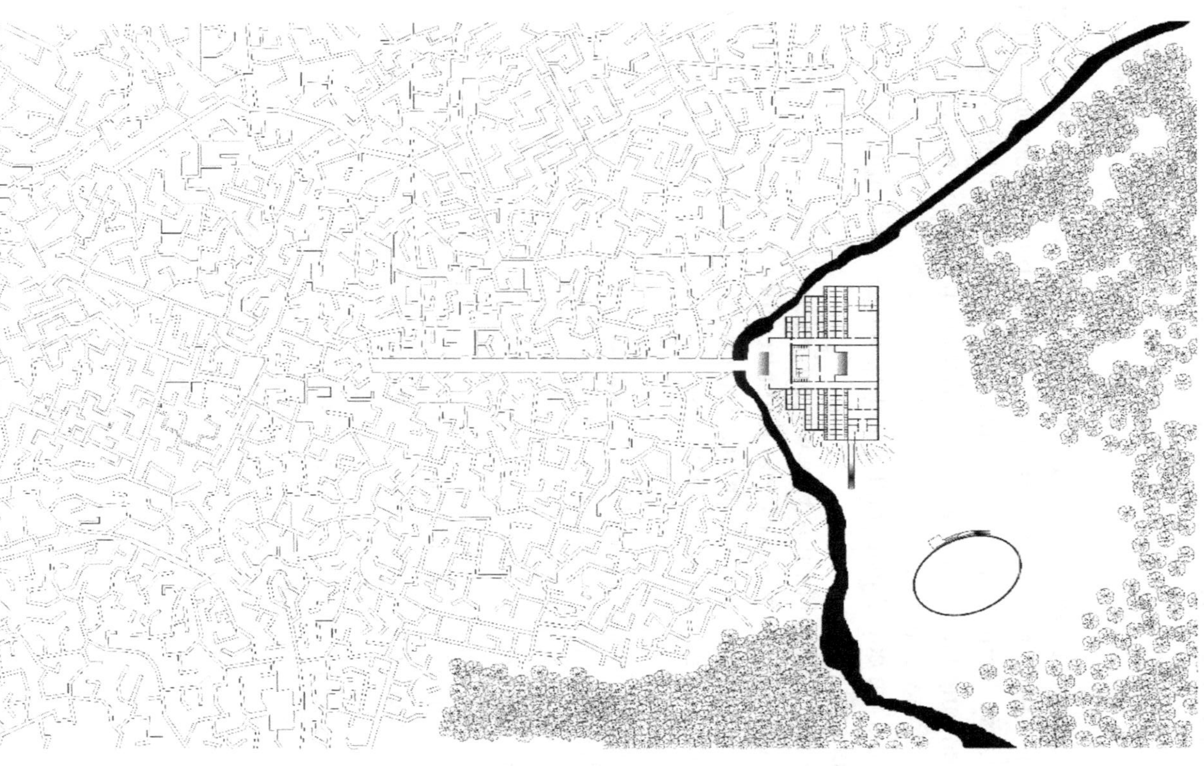

MAP OF HELL

CHAPTER ONE

In retrospect, we should have known better. I mean – c'mon now! – nobody's trying to get into Hell. It's the one place everybody tries to stay away from. This whole thing had "wrong" written all over it in sixteen languages. At least sixteen, though I doubt any were in the lexicon of the military.

I guess we could just chalk another one up for "military intelligence".

The first I heard of this was when General "Ironguts" Strittmeier was announced as the speaker at that afternoon's briefing. Being a big fan, I thought I would capture him on video for my buddies back in the unit and maybe even get the man's autograph, time and opportunity permitting.

After the little get together had started, I realized how foolish it was to be recording the meeting. But, hey, nobody told me it was hush-hush until the General's opening remarks. By that time, I was too scared to shut the damned thing off.

Do I still have it? Of course!

I may have been too frightened to shut it off but after that I was too frightened to erase it. This was something that might have had some huge historical ramifications and I wanted to keep it for the historical record. Well, that and possible sale to that television show about homemade videos.

The story is so unbelievable that I suppose I should show you some of the introduction I had to the whole mess. It sounded rather simple an assignment – bizarre, yes, but simple – but that was before we actually confronted the crazy situation.

RECORDING, START *16APR2028:1635*

"…nty a pleasure to you, General Strittmeier, who is in charge of this mission."

Sounds of chairs scuffling, minor muttering. The General strode into the frame as silence fell over the room. He squared his shoulders and stared around the room.

"Afternoon, gentlemen. We have a critical situation and we need volunteers. If anyone objects to this mission on religious or any other grounds, I will ask you to leave the room. If what you hear offends or disgusts you in any way, I ask you to leave the room as quietly as possible. Is that understood?"

He turned his head to the right.

"No questions, son. If anyone hears something personally objectionable, leave as soon as that decision is made. And remember: everything that is presented in this room is strictly confidential. I do not want to hear it spoken of beyond the confines of mission space. I do not want to see it mentioned on the internet. I do not want to see it on your Facebook updates. I do not want to see it on the evening news. I do not even want to read about it in the pages of some science fiction thriller. Is that understood?

"Good. You are probably wondering how you can decide if this mission is for you without hearing the particulars. I prefaced my briefing with those rules so that as we proceed through the particulars, if any one of you suddenly finds yourself unable to commit yourself wholeheartedly to the success of this venture, I want you to leave at that point.

"There will be no repercussions for departure. As I said, this is a voluntary situation, for reasons that will become clear as we proceed. Is that understood? Good. Major, would you get the lights?"

The lights dimmed and a projector illuminated a screen at the front of the room behind the General.

"This is an image taken a week ago in St. Peter's Square, in the Vatican City, in Rome. The pictures you are about to see may be too much for some of you.

"There was an explosion at this site a week ago. Subsequent investigation has led many to believe it was the act of terrorists. As the vehicle for the explosion was a device containing anti-matter, it was given the highest priority. If anyone is unfamiliar with the concept, anti-matter reacts violently when it contacts regular matter. The resultant explosion seems to have opened a trans-dimensional rift – a doorway, if you will. This doorway is unstable in its present form but it is being held open only through the efforts of someone, or some *thing*, on the other side.

"Once this was discovered, scientists from the Fermi Institute in Italy have determined how the portal was being kept open and have applied the same technique from this dimension. And why did they do this? Look.

"Many cultures throughout the history of mankind have spoken of this place and our modern understanding was that the place was nothing more than myth, and bad mythology, at that. Gentlemen, what you are looking at is an entryway into nothing less than Hell itself.

"Now, while the scientists and theologians debate whether this is real, or some such poppycock, we have been entrusted with the very explicit directive of removing the threat that Hell poses to humankind. Here you see a variety of demon forms. And here is what we believe is Satan himself, seated on his throne."

Sounds of chairs moving on the floor and footsteps leaving.

"Not for the weak-willed as you can see. And not for the faint of heart. Look good at it, misters, and heed all the warnings given in Holy Writ since time began. This monstrosity is behind all the evils in the world today. I don't care if they find out how these bullies have tortured mankind for ages, I intend to put an end to it.

"For the first time in human history, Hell is finally available to us in this life, not simply after death when your soul is too weak to match the powers of darkness.

"At last we can stop the insinuation of the demons in our daily world. We can take the fight to Satan himself.

"Some people are referring to these creatures as demons but I find that has far too many religious connotations to be of any practical use so I call them ‘lobsters' because that is the color they are. The Brits in the American Revolution were called lobster-backs, and we will use that same mentality. No need to humanize them at all. Remember: these are aliens, and not the friendly cuddly sort of ET we had hoped for.

"The first recon team to go in were three Roman policemen and a cameraman. He was the one you can thank for the images. May his soul rest in heaven, if it ever makes it there. The policemen found out their guns would not work. One even used his suspenders to launch a bullet at the lobsters but it seemed to only become absorbed by the demon.

"Lead doesn't hurt them and gunpowder does not react chemically in that realm. What a subsequent group found was that stainless steel crossbow bolts seem to do the trick. A third team went in armed with crossbows and held off the lobsters long enough to find a chemical reaction that would work there.

"From that, we have developed ordnance for you to use there. It is not as powerful as what you're used to but it's the best we've been able to come up with at the moment. Anyone slow on the trigger will end up like this guy."

Retching is heard; more chairs scuffling and feet leaving the room. When the noise ended, the General continued.

"One of their primary defenses is playing with your mind – not a stretch if you think about their history in that regard – and so any troops in the field will use special headsets. It surrounds your head with white noise, three-sixty. You will have the opportunity to practice with these headsets before we enter the belly of the beast. The one thing you must remember while using them is DO NOT THINK. Don't even try to. You are well-trained killing machines and that is all you will have to do. Commanders will have override capability to get the orders to you through the noise but you will have to do as your commander directs. If you find that you can still think with the white-noise, we can crank it up. It seems some people are more tolerant of it." He grinned. "I wonder why? Maybe from shutting out people whose talking annoyed you, perhaps. But don't play games with this, mister. A single soldier who falls victim to the aliens' mind control can take out his entire unit. So be vigilant."

More chairs moving could be heard. Then the General surveyed the room.

"My compliments, Major, of the forty-seven that began the meeting, we still have sixteen remaining. Do I understand then that you gentlemen wish to volunteer for this mission?"

He looked intent. "So, who's with me?" Hands went up.

"Okay, then. Very good. Major, see that these men are sent to Qualcomm Two immediately."

The General left the frame.

RECORDING, END *16APR2028:1645*

I was shaking like a leaf. I had just recorded a secret briefing. Was I scared about getting caught? Does a duck have webbed feet and go quackers? You bet your flabby ass I was! But I wasn't about to bail on what was probably going to be the biggest and most important battle in the history of mankind.

I left that tape behind and carried a fresh one on the mission – you know, hoping to catch some of the sights and sounds of the mission – but the damned thing didn't work there. I lost it in one of the skirmishes.

Yeah, I wondered how the demons had been able to cross over and manipulate our ancestors, but that was not my main concern. Mine was how can you kill the ugly bastards?

And I had a sneaking suspicion that once you got the ugly suckers annihilated that it might just take a little more effort to keep them that way. Maybe I had just played a few too many video games in my time or maybe I was feeling a trap, I don't know, but if these guys were the worst nightmare mankind had experienced for millennia and they played by a different set of rules, anything was possible.

After a very rushed packing – not much really left to pack when your status is "active" – my thoughts ranged all over the map while taking the sardine express to Qualcomm Two. From the cramped quarters of the transport, one would have thought the General was expecting fewer volunteers than he actually got. And that thought got me to wondering what he had neglected to tell us. If he had expected a smaller number, either he did not know his men – a highly unlikely prospect for old "Ironguts" – or there were a few details he had inadvertently left out of his lecture. Or perhaps he left them out on purpose.

Anyway, that night before turning in, I hit the internet to see what I could find on the demonic realm and ways to combat them. Quite naturally, there was not a viable plan for any such combat. Since rational people refused to acknowledge the reality of such a place as Satan's realm, the only websites holding court on the issue were those a little further into the lunatic fringe than I was accustomed to venturing. But as I was about to invade a mythical realm, I was willing to look for help from any quarter.

I did not know whether to laugh, cry, or run screaming into the dark night pulling my hair out. How could supposedly rational human beings think such bizarre things? Still, a week before I would have thought the idea of invading the physical realm we know as

Hell would have been the delusional pastime of some of the more radical of the priesthood.

I remembered the old stories about using silver bullets against werewolves and wooden stakes against vampires. Not your traditional ordnance but something to keep firmly in mind with the dimensional differences. Perhaps, I thought, I should arm myself with garlic, holy water, and crucifixes.

The closest I could come up with was video games. I had spent a lot of time playing those when I was younger. Mainly first-person-shooters – and I remembered some of them had story lines similar to this mission. Reviewing those didn't help much because ordnance worked fine there. You shot a demon and he went down. Bigger ones required bigger guns, but they didn't just absorb the bullets… they died.

The search was fruitless and I was a bit annoyed that there had never been any serious studies put into the subject since about the twelfth century or so. But then most people assumed it was just some religious myth, despite all the ghost-hunters and exorcists over the centuries.

I fell asleep that first night with the visions of sugar plump demons dancing menacingly on my grave and awoke in a cold sweat.

CHAPTER TWO

Qualcomm Two was out in the middle of nowhere, so don't ask me. Nobody told me where we were and I didn't ask. The one day I was there, I was too busy to worry about any of that. Hell, I could've been on Mars for all I knew.

We had already been assigned into units and the roster had us fall into those groups. I checked the roster and ran to find the tent we had been assigned.

"Hey, fresh meat!" One of the guys in the tent announced my arrival. He shoved a hand at me. "Hank Ferguson, from Iowa by way of the 101st."

I slid my pack to the ground. "Eric Patterson." I shook the offered hand. Introductions went quickly. Tom Huff was a short stocky kid from New York, Ronny Griffin, a California boy nearly as lanky as Ferguson, Vernon Chou, who seemed to be some sorta math whiz kid from Boston, Derrick Kowalski from Houston, Danny Garcia of Arizona, who always seemed to be smiling, Ricky Vaudelet, an intense and nervous kid from the Midwest, and Bennett Wainwright, who seemed to be an intellectual from Seattle.

All of us were from different units. The guys I knew from the first briefing must have all been assigned other units here. That happens a lot. Before we got too comfortable, this giant of a fellow walked in. Everyone snapped to attention. He saluted before a grin spread across his black face.

"At ease, men. I am Sergeant Miller and I will be corralling you young mustangs for the duration of this mission. Lieutenant Ordway will be along shortly to meet you, as soon as the brass has finished chatting the officers up." His eyes narrowed and he looked us over. "This mission is supposed to be 'different' from anything we've encountered before but I think you all know it's the same ol' same ol'. We go in and make their body count be higher than ours. We get to the objective and take it out." He smirked. "Doesn't matter if they're using men, cattle, robots, or demons. It's the same ol' same ol'. Keep your heads down, follow orders, and we'll all make it back to crack open the brewskies. You got it?"

We answered as one. "Yes, sir!"

He grinned. "Now, let's get out to the range and see what kind of firepower they've got for us, huh?"

We walked out of the tent and down the packed dirt pathway between tents where other soldiers were getting the same pep talk. Over a rise, we saw the firing range. Several other squads were already in position firing at the targets, and we moved along to the end of the firing line where positions were unoccupied. Another Sergeant was waiting for us there.

"Good morning, gentlemen. I am Sergeant Morgan and I will be instructing you in the use of the ordnance you will be using for this mission. Thank you, Sergeant Miller, I'll send your ducklings back when they've learned to swim."

Miller grinned, saluted casually, and looked us over again. "Listen up, fellas. If you can't master this part of the program, you will find no place on the transport." He motioned with a finger pointing downward. "*This* training is vital to our success." His dark face grew intense for a moment before easing back into the grin. "I'll see you when you've finished here."

"Listen to your Sergeant, fellows," Morgan drew our attention back to him. "This may be an easy transition for some of you but those of you who are too set in your ways may have a difficult time. Yes, son?"

Huff had raised his hand. "Sorry, sir, but I heard that it was going to be something completely new. I see the other guys shooting what looks like M-16's."

"That's right, son. And that's what's going to be tricky for some of you. The Army didn't have time to create any new weaponry for this mission. What they did make was new ordnance to fit what we had available. Since you are used to firing the weapon, you need to get used to how this stuff works. And believe me, it works differently." He reached in a pocket and pulled out a bullet. "Looks like pretty standard stuff, don't it? 'Cept that this generation has a stainless steel casing and the charge that sets it off is not any explosive you're used to." He placed the shell back in his pocket. "Any of you ever use baking soda and vinegar when you were kids to make an explosion?" He looked around, saw a few nods. "Well, this ain't exactly that combination but that's the closest thing I can think of that it resembles. It's slow." He shook his head. "No, that's not quite right. It's damned slow! You'll notice when you fire the weapon that there is a pause before it fires and it doesn't have any kickback to speak of." He looked around. "That said, you ain't gonna really get it until you try it. So, everyone grab a rifle and let's try it out." He motioned toward a teepee rack of rifles.

Each of us grabbed a weapon and stood along the line, strung out about fifty yards from the targets.

"Fire at will."

I raised the rifle, took aim, and pulled the trigger. It was the weirdest feeling. It's like nothing happened… not for the longest time. I was just about to pull it down and check to see if the trigger had jammed, when it fired. It startled me. I suddenly understood what people meant when they said things got pear-shaped. The sensation was just… well, weird!

I aimed and fired again. This time, I paid more attention to the timing and realized it wasn't really that long a delay. Your training tells you when the weapon does not respond instantly that something must be wrong. It was going to take a while to get over that instinct. And that must be what this exercise was for.

Glancing to the side, I noticed a couple of the guys seemed to adapt instantly. Ferguson and Wainwright were firing slow and steady. And then there was the other sort. Vaudelet almost shot himself in the head. He had fired like me but, when nothing happened immediately, he pulled the weapon down to try and look into the barrel to see if it was jammed. And of course, that's when it discharged.

It's a good thing he wasn't quick enough or he'd've blown his head off. Sergeant Morgan ducked and screamed at him.

I mean, what sort of fool looks down the barrel of a loaded weapon? Everyone moved a little away from the guy at that point.

The Sarge came over to talk him down and walk him through it slowly.

"Take it easy, son. You have to remember the bullet exits the chamber at a slower speed. That means you have to keep it sighted on your target a second more than usual."

Vaudelet lowered his voice. "Sorry, sir, but I thought it was jammed."

"That's okay. Try it again."

Ricky raised the rifle and fired again. This time, he held the pose until it discharged.

"That's better, son. Remember: squeeze and hold."

Before the Sergeant moved down the line, I lowered my weapon. "Excuse me, sir. What sort of weapons do the demons… er, lobsters have?"

The Sarge turned and looked around, speaking loud enough for all of us to hear. "Son, I don't know about this 'lobster' talk. They're demons, so I say we just call them demons. That's my take on it. Now, about what they use. All they seem to have is some sort of rock launcher."

Ferguson stepped closer. "Did you say 'rocket launchers'?" He looked at his rifle. "How are these supposed to hold up against that?"

"No, not 'rocket launchers', *rock* launchers. And apparently with all the rubble over there, they have plenty of ammo."

Ferguson looked relieved. Griffin scratched his head. "Don't seem like throwing rocks at us is going to slow us down too much."

Sarge grinned an evil grin. "Kid, did you ever hear tell a story about David and Goliath?" A lot of the guys grinned. "Well, these rocks are going to be going quite a bit faster and some of 'em are going to be a damned sight larger. You may think it's a bit primitive for our standards but remember that you are going onto their home turf here. And they've had a lot more practice with their rocks than you've had with these things. One good thing, though, is if the thing misses you it can't do any damage. They don't have anything like grenades. So, let's get back to it."

Griffin stared at his rifle. "But, sir, with us having to stand still so long, won't they get us while we're waiting for this damned thing to fire?"

"Movement. You have to learn to move around while maintaining a lock on your target. You won't have to maintain it for more than a second but you have to get used to the timing. If you're a target for one of them you have to be able to fire, and move while maintaining the aim on your target. So, let's get back to the practice."

We all went back to the line more focused than before. His little chat had made it seem a lot more real that even these primitive-seeming demons could present a dangerous situation to any of us. The world seemed a little less "pear-shaped" to me.

But his estimate of the enemies' capabilities was a little bit off. They may not have grenades, exactly, but a large rock hitting a wall tends to send a cascade of rubble as bad as any grenade would have. Knowing the capabilities of their own weapons made them a lot more dangerous than we were led to believe.

And Vaudelet still seemed to be having trouble. "Shit! This thing doesn't work!" He looked up to see Sarge. "Oops! Sorry, sir."

"You're still trying too hard, soldier. Try it again. Hold the aim on your target, pull the trigger slowly, and hold it there until the weapon fires."

He tried it again while the Sarge watched. He hit the target.

"That's better, soldier. With more practice you'll get used to the timing."

The guy nodded. "Thanks, Sarge. I think I'm getting it."

"I hope so, son." And he moved on down the line.

I figure we were there more than an hour, firing, reloading, and firing some more. After I had gotten used to the timing, I worked on moving side to side or ducking while maintaining aspect on the target.

It was damned hard. Harder than I thought it would be but we had years of training to override. That I was able to do it at all I give credit to some wicked videogames I had played that used similar tactics. Of course it was a bit harder in real life as you could not simply hold the "Control" key while you hit the "Space Bar", but you get my drift.

After we had become comfortable with it, the targets were laid down and we shot at a farther group. And later, an even farther group. At a hundred-fifty yards, the things were practically useless. We had to aim well above the target to hit anything and, when the wind blew at all, the shots went wide.

We struggled with it but I think we finally got it.

As we were re-racking the rifles, Vaudelet commented, "A couple more days at this and I think I'll have it."

Sarge grinned like a demon. "Sorry to disappoint you, soldier, but that's the extent of it. You only get this one day."

Vaudelet did not release the rifle. "One day?" He looked around at the rest of us. "Can we stay a little longer then? I'm still not comfortable with it."

"You can come back later," the Sarge waved them along, "but there's other stuff you have to know as well. Anyone who still needs practice can come back after dinner."

We tramped back along the line where most of the earlier groups had already rotated out for fresh units. Up the rise, we were turned over to Sergeant Miller again while another unit came down to take the place we had just vacated.

"Anything to report?"

Sergeant Morgan shook his head. "They're a fine bunch and nobody shot anyone, so I'd say it went okay." He glanced at Vaudelet, who reddened. "A few might need to come back after dinner to hone their technique but I'd said they're ready to go."

"Very good. Come along, men."

We quick-stepped back along the pathway between tents, past our own and onward to the mess tent, set up across the pathway at the end of the compound. Guys were leaving as we arrived. One shift going out and another coming in.

We got in the chow line and then followed Sarge with our trays to a table, where the Lieutenant was already eating. We surrounded the table and saluted.

"At ease, men. Eat."

We sat and dug in.

"I am Lieutenant Ordway." He finished his meal as we began eating ours, wiped his mouth with a napkin and sat back. "I hear you've done well with your training so far and that's a good thing. I've been in training, myself, for the better part of two days now. Command has designed a battle plan and we've outlined the strategies we'll be using." He leaned forward, his elbows resting on the edge of the table. "These are not your typical enemies, by any stretch of the imagination, but they are still the enemy. Knowing them and using that knowledge, we can prevail. So we will have to learn all we can in any encounter with them. Anything we observe can be used to help us defeat them." He leaned back again.

"There is no complete map of the area we are going into. We can't do a reconnaissance fly-over to show us what to expect, so we are going to have to create a map in real-time to let command know what we are up against. After your meal, we will get into the nuts and bolts of the mission and what you can expect in the operation." He stood and held up a hand. "As you were, gentlemen." Looking at

Sarge, he nodded. "Bring them back to the tent when you've finished here."

"Yes, sir."

"And I'll see you men shortly."

After he had gone, Griffin spoke up. "Sarge, what was he saying about some changes we can expect? What else is going on here?"

"Soldier, why don't we just wait and let the Lieutenant show us in his own way?"

"Yes, sir."

The remainder of the meal passed quickly and in silence. No one had any clue what else we had to learn before the mission and no one seemed ready to open their mouth and look the fool while the Sergeant was there.

After eating, we dumped off the trays and double-timed it back to our tent where we found the Lieutenant talking with another officer. We took up places around the tent and stood at ease.

"Men," the Lieutenant stood and stepped to the side, "I'm going to turn things over to Captain Hartsock here to tell you about the other equipment you will be using. Captain."

Hartsock held up a helmet that had wires dangling from it. "Gentlemen, this piece of equipment may do more to save your lives than anything else you possess. It is assumed the demons use some form of mind-control over their enemies. Apparently that's how they have worked over the centuries and they are probably even more adept at it on their own turf. And this nifty little device acts as a buffer against such attacks."

One of the fellows, I think it was Griffin, raised his hand. "Sir, how will we know for certain that it is them manipulating our minds?"

"Soldier, we are not even certain that is what they do but it seems likely. And how will you know if it is happening? Probably when you get the sudden urge to shoot your platoon leader, I suppose." Everyone laughed at that, though it was an uneasy sort of laugh. "Any thought that seems out of the ordinary to you, you gotta figure is being put into your head by the demons. We are not exactly certain what they are capable of but you need to be prepared for anything."

He raised the helmet again. "This contraption sets up a small energy field around your head to interfere with a wide variety of wavelengths. Hopefully, the ones the demons could be using. It is just what they call 'white noise' and won't interfere with your ability to think or talk normally." He lowered it and looked around at all of us. "The primary problem with these devices is that it creates some interference with normal radio communication as well. Only the squad leader will have the necessary equipment to override the headset and communicate with HQ. And they should use it sparingly to reduce the possibility of demonic interference." His look was hard. "Got it?"

There were yessirs from the group. Wainwright nudged me with an elbow and leaned close. "I can just see the Lieutenant opening the comm circuit and getting his brain fried. I guess we're supposed to be on guard for any strange orders, huh?"

The Captain nodded, having heard the comment. In that small space, I think everybody heard it.

"That's right men. If your squad leader starts giving some strange orders, you'll know to keep your guard up. That's why they will be cautioned to use the comm channels only in emergency situations. We don't want to lose anyone to demon mind control."

Sergeant Miller spoke up. "Each unit is going in as an independent unit. We hope to cover all the bases in this training to prevent having to contact HQ at all. Only if something unexpected happens will the Lieutenant make contact. Otherwise, we do our mission and get out." He grinned. "And we don't need a lot of brass breathing down our necks anyway, do we?"

"That's right, fellas." Hartsock nodded. "Each of the units is expected to have enough training to preclude needing to use the radio at all. But we like to cover our butts whenever possible. Another thing," he held up some goggles, "these are to counteract the orange glow that permeates the region. After a time you would suffer something akin to snowblindness. It should filter out a lot of the orangeness and keep your vision clear."

He stepped aside to display a crate behind him. "I want each of you to come forward and take a helmet and a pair of these eyewear. Try 'em out, get used to them. They may be the things that will save your butt when we get over there."

Everyone donned the new equipment. There were no dangling wires from the helmets we got but you could see the electronics imbedded in the lining. Still, it wasn't noticeable after you put it on.

When everyone had the gear set, the Captain spoke again. "This here on the back of the headgear," he pointed to the small spot, "turns the white noise on and off. We intentionally put it on the back so it would be harder to accidentally shut it off. Like I said, it is to be kept on all the time, except for the squad leader and only in emergencies." He glanced around to make sure everyone was ready. "Okay, now. I want each of you to push that button now and turn the headset on."

I reached to the back of my helmet and, looking at the back of Wainwright's for direction, located the button and pushed. I don't know what I was expecting – maybe a low humming noise or a buzzing – but there was nothing. No noticeable change.

"Does anybody hear a difference?"

I looked around to see everyone shaking their head: no.

The Captain grinned. "Good, it works."

Funniest thing, I was thinking what if this thing was nothing more than a placebo. You know, something that let us think it was working when it wasn't doing anything. And since no one I knew of could send thought messages to me, I had no way of knowing if the thing was on or off.

"Sir," I just had to know, "I can't hear anything different. So how do we know if the unit is on or off? Or if the battery dies or something."

"Look up."

Everyone's head jerked up.

"No, not at the ceiling. Look up to the edge of your helmet."

I looked up and at the edge of my vision was a small LED growing red.

"That small light will tell you the unit is working. We didn't want to put it in a more visible location in case it would help show the enemy your position. But you should be able to see it well enough." He looked around. "Any more questions?"

I had about a gazillion more but I guessed they could wait. Without enough information, it was impossible to even think of an intelligent question.

Or was that just the white noise interfering with my thought processes?

That was a scary thought.

*****

The Captain left us after that and the Sarge let us walk around and get used to the new equipment, such as it was. Several of the guys said they could hear the gizmo working but I didn't get any of that. Without looking up to check the little light, I had no idea when it was on or off.

At least we did not have to go through the extra training to learn how to override the thing to make radio contact. Just the thought of shutting the unit off when in enemy territory – even for a split second – gave me the shivers.

Vaudelet and a couple of other guys went back to the firing range to get more practice on the weapons while the rest of us sat around the tent.

"Sarge?" Ferguson spoke. "Does this mean an end to the need for soldiers?"

"What are you talking about, son?"

"Well, I figure the demons are the ones who make people want to do crazy things, like the terrorism and such, so won't that sort of stop when the demons are wiped out? Will there even need to be an army afterwards or are we going to put ourselves out of work?"

The Sergeant leaned back and thought a moment. "I don't know exactly what influence the demons have had over the centuries, son, but I figure Man is capable of doing some pretty nasty shit all on his own."

"Do you mean the demons only cause the big problems?" Huff looked ill at ease. "Or do they do the little things as well?"

Garcia responded. "My grandmother said demons can make people react on their meaner instincts. Greed, envy, lust… those sorts of things."

"Yeah," Huff considered a moment, "but isn't that the sorts of things that have always led to war? Greed and… what's the word? Coveting?"

"I really don't think," Sergeant Miller leaned forward, "that we can really answer any of these questions. Nor do I think we have to. But it's my own opinion that 'the devil made me do it' is an out a lot of people use when it really has nothing to do with anything more than their pride." He nodded toward Garcia. "Or their greed or envy.

These seem to be rather basic human instincts and originally, I should think, they were things that led to our survival." He shrugged. "In some people – an unbalanced few, perhaps – it just gets out of hand."

Private Chou laughed. "I can see that well enough. When a pretty girl walks by, it is not the chattering of some demon that sparks my interest."

"Maybe so," Ferguson was not amused, "but how will it affect things like terrorism? That certainly can't be some natural instinct, Sarge. Some of the things coming out of that are just plain evil."

"Well, evil, like beauty, is in the eye of the beholder. I doubt if a suicide bomber is thinking their act is anything less than heroism. That's simply confusion, or a difference of opinion, not the devil." He stood up. "Seems like all of you feel pretty comfortable with the new ordnance, huh?" There were nods and "yessirs". Sarge grinned. "Okay, fellas, lets go out and try to hit the targets while running."

So, we did not have the afternoon off as some of the guys were probably thinking and I guess it was a good thing to keep us at it. Sarge must have remembered the old saying about idle hands being the Devil's workshop and we certainly didn't need them coming to us. We would go to meet them when we were ready.

CHAPTER THREE

We were rolled out of bed at oh-dark-thirty, an ungodly hour to be doing anything except sawing logs. But like most guys, I could get active when need be and sleep on my feet later if I had to. Even during a twenty-miler, I could catch a few zee's before the drill sergeant came back along the line to where I was.

You learned to count on your instinct to tell you when to come around again. Guys who either didn't have such a sense or could not utilize it had no business being in the military. Without that basic survival instinct, your next residence was bound to be a body-bag.

If we had thought the flight to Europe was going to be more pleasurable, we had a rather rude awakening. This transport was even more cramped than the ride to Qualcomm Two. We were grouped by squad, sitting with Sergeant Miller, but there was no real division between the various groups on board. Like I said, it was cramped.

Wainwright was sitting next to me and he seemed a little too calm. The other guys seemed a little nervous about venturing into the unknown, but he was the real cool cucumber of the group.

Several of the guys were trying to make enough room to get a game of cards going and not having a lot of luck. I was just about to join them when Wainwright spoke to no one in particular.

"Demons are a lot like vampires, you know."

Looking around, I couldn't figure out who the comment was meant for. I shrugged mentally – there was no room to do it physically – and responded: "How do you figure?"

He grinned. "Demons can't just enter our realm anytime they want; they have to be invited. Someone has to call them; haven't you ever heard of 'summoning a demon'? It's like that."

"I hadn't given it much thought."

"It's true." He nodded. "I am not exactly certain how the inter-dimensional transfer works, but I'm pretty sure they don't have free access."

"And how do you know so much about it? Are you in a coven or something?"

He turned as well as he could in those cramped quarters. "Heck no! I'm a Catholic. And the nuns're always warning us to be wary of the influence of demons. They said if you lowered your guard and thought about sinning, that was as good as summoning them."

"Huh." I shook my head. "I was raised Methodist. I don't think they even believe in demons."

Griffin leaned forward on the other side of Wainwright to join the discussion. "I was raised Pentecostal and we don't seem to be any better informed than the Methodists. What can we expect from these guys?"

Now, suddenly, it appeared one of our own had become an expert on demons.

"I don't know for sure. It's not like anyone's done a scientific study on the subject. But if the legends are anywhere near correct, they can warp your minds and get you to do the worst things ever. But first you have to want to use them and their powers."

"But, wait." I was having trouble with his thinking. "If you have to invite them in, how can they control our minds or anything?"

"I think once you decide you require their assistance in whatever it is you want to achieve – wealth, fame, power, or even lust – you have opened the gate for them to come in but you also open your mind to their influence. If your mind is already so warped, I don't suppose you would even notice it getting even more warped, would you?"

"So, they're like the poor relations you invite to stay for a couple of days and they never leave." Griffin grinned. "I've got cousins like that."

"I think that's the way it works."

I just had to know. "So you've been studying demons your whole life? And the Catholics know all about them?" I was beginning to think maybe the demons had a better foothold in this world than we credited them. I mean, they did come up right in front of the Vatican, fer chrissakes.

"No, actually, my mother doesn't believe in demons at all. Hell, yes, demons, no. She thinks bad people do bad things just because they are bent." He shook his head. "It is not a part of the religion to put great store in demons but the subject has always fascinated me. I read a lot about them."

I mentioned the research I had attempted on the internet.

"Yeah, you're right about that. There has not been any serious studies in the subject since the Age of Reason took over. It has all been relegated to myth."

Griffith grunted. "I guess this gives that theory a black-eye."

Wainwright shook his head. "But it still makes no sense."

"Whatcha mean?"

He looked from the front of the plane to the back. "General Strittmeier said that it was the presence of evil that caused people to go to war and yet here we are, rational human beings, going to war to end war." He shook his head. "But if it is the demons who make us want to war, who is making us go to this war? Wouldn't it be the demons?"

"That doesn't make any sense." Griffith shook his head. "No sense at all."

"Do you mean," I asked slowly, "that you suspect the demons are controlling us to invade Hell? You think they want us to attack them? Why?"

Cocking his head to one side, he chewed on a lip for a moment before answering. "I'm not certain of their reasons, but couldn't it be that they want us to invade? After all, the General said someone over there was keeping the portal open. I want to know why."

"Like a trap?"

He shrugged or tried to.

Ferguson had been listening and now leaned forward. "What are you doing here, then, if you don't believe in the mission? And why are you in the Army if you think demons are really running the show?"

"I just cannot think of another way to keep the world safe."

I nodded. "Me too. I just want to rid the world of the bad guys so my children and grandchildren can grow up in peace. I figure getting the demons out of the mix is a good idea."

"Yeah, but who's the good guys and bad guys?" Wainwright wanted to know.

Again, I tried to shrug but couldn't move. "It's not intended to be philosophical. I figure anyone that opposes what I believe is a bad guy to my mind."

He nodded again. "Yep, that about sums it up for everyone. We all are fighting against what we think is wrong. I don't really see anything demonic influencing that."

Griffin still looked worried. "But you don't know for sure?"

"Like I said, it's not a science. Maybe things work differently when you're in their world."

Relaxing a bit, Griffin nodded. "Yeah. The General said things work differently over there. Maybe that's part of it."

"Well, we'll just have to wait and see."

We were quiet a while as I mulled over what he had said. He did not seem to know more about demons than the rest of us but what he said about their influence maybe behind this whole adventure just seemed… well, wrong.

We were doing this for the right reasons, weren't we?

Not just because "the devil made me do it".

The heat was raining down like a bear on the paved square in front of St. Peter's Cathedral. I jumped down from the back of the APC and fell into line with the rest of the troops. Quite a few stopped before hitting formation to kneel and bow their head toward the basilica and then cross themselves.

I thought most of the really religious types – those more so than Wainwright and the few who were chatting on the transport – had bailed during the opening lecture on this operation but I guess there were a few from some of the other bases who came along for the incursion. Either that or more than a few of the fellows had "got religion" on their way to the staging area. Soon, though, the several hundred of us were arranged by squad in front of Ironguts.

While the brass chit-chatted among themselves and we sweated in the hot August afternoon sunshine, I glanced at the jagged opening into the next dimension thrust up through the pavement of the plaza like some compound fracture I had seen before. Surrounding it were several parabolic dishes and a half-dozen generators the size of boxcars. Probably to run power cables into Hell to run radios, lights, and the odd DVD television set, I assumed.

And there had been a strange change since the video had been shot for our indoc purposes. The slightly orange tinge to the paving stones and soil that had been apparent surrounding the immediate area of the intrusion had now spread beyond the immediate area of disruption. It now extended some three or four feet beyond the trans-dimensional vortex.

I wondered idly if that had been just a fault of the recording equipment or if the discoloration was actually spreading? And could it be the proximity to the nether region that was making the air around us so damned hot? Or was Rome really this warm in August? I had been through Desert Storm II and the sweltering deserts of Iraq but that seemed a pleasant picnic compared to this heat.

Finally, the brass finished patting each other on the back and got down to business.

Ironguts turned to face us, shoulders squared, hands clenched together behind his back. "Men, I am sure you all have been adequately briefed on the situation here and the use of the new weapons we have to use in the realm we are about to enter. Since we are not entirely certain of their operational measures or their intentions, we must assume the worst.

"So, men, are you ready for the adventure of a lifetime? I guarantee you that each and every one of you will go down in history for what we do here today." One of the team raised a hand. "Yes, soldier?"

"Sir, what about non-combatants? Do we know of any?"

Ironguts grinned. "From where I see it, a lobster's a lobster, whether it's trying to rip your head off or not. There are no non-combatants to worry about. Every 'thing' you encounter will be an enemy." Another hand. "Yes?"

"Sir, I have heard the demons can play with your mind. How will we know it's affecting us?"

The general's eyes narrowed as he looked around at the officers. "Who was in charge of this lad's training?" When no answer was forthcoming, "Soldier, fall out until you can be briefed properly. Now are there any others who do not fully understand what we're up against?"

There were no takers. He continued, "You will get in there and establish a beachhead before we insert the second wave." He unfurled a street map behind him. "This is all we have in the way of a map, boys, so learn it well. Here," he pointed to an area at the left of the map, "is our insertion point. The gateway opening you saw over there in the square opens directly onto this spot.

"You may experience a small degree of disorientation on entering their world because the level of their world is tilted some fifteen degrees to ours. Looking through the doorway, it appears you are on top of a hill and the city is downhill from you. It is not down from you, it is on the level. Some think-tank boys are working on why this is so but I think it really has no bearing on our mission.

"Which is," he pointed to a large structure on the right of the map, "this palace building over here. This is the seat of Satan himself, where he appears to reside and is the surest place to find the bastard. We move in here and blast it from existence.

"Some of the locals do not seem to attack at once but that is probably because they are waiting for reinforcements or they plan something sneakier than a frontal assault. Kill them quickly and move on."

"Sir!"

"Yes, son? A question?"

"Yes, sir. The side streets don't show on the map, sir. Are they all that short?"

Ironguts turned to look at the map a moment. The map showed the longer streets but only the beginnings of the side streets. "Oh, I see. The map was made while under attack and as they did not venture along any side passages, we are only certain of the roadways the recon team actually went. The first couple of streets nearer the entrance can be seen to be cul-de-sacs, and another couple cut through to somewhere.

"Use whatever routes you can to get to this area," he made a circle on the map, "as there is a large and straight road here leading directly to the palace. Our troops will come from the entry point, in a two-prong attack to reach this road." He put his hands on his hips. "And then," he grinned, "our superior firepower will show those lobsters who's boss. Right?"

"Yes, sir!" the men chorused.

"Two things you must remember. First," he raised a pair of goggles that hung around his neck, "wear your goggles at all times. The orange glow that permeates Hell will give you something akin to snow-blindness without them. And, two, make sure your helmets are in working order. Check those of your squad and make sure they check yours. We don't want to lose any man through that type of interference. Now, everyone ready?"

"Yes, sir!"

"Then let's go get 'em, boys!"

There was no fanfare or applause and the general turned us over to the squad leaders.

Three platoons were called to attention and moved off toward the orangey glow. One of the three was the one I was in and, as we approached the opening, the other two came to a halt while we proceeded.

Somehow, I had gotten lucky enough to be in the group that would establish that beachhead the General was talking about. I suppose it was an honor to be in that group but it was also a little daunting. I wondered exactly how long we were going to have to hold the demons at bay before the second squad came in?

And what if we did not hold?

Lieutenant Ordway stopped beside the opening and turned to face us. "Ready, men?" Then he reached to the back of his helmet. "Helmets on!" We each reached back and turned our own devices on and I glanced upward to make sure the red LED was on. "Goggles!" He donned his eyewear and we followed suit. "All right, Sergeant, let's get them in." He turned and ducked through the opening.

I gulped once and stepped after the guy in front of me and we drew closer to the opening, the orange getting a bit more intense as we approached. I slipped the goggles on, then I ducked my head and stepped into another world.

CHAPTER FOUR

The footing was difficult, to say the least. It was like we were set down on a slope of rubble, loose rock from a collapsed building. After taking a few uneasy steps, I turned to look back at the opening. Weird! From the other side it had been outlined completely by the paving stones of the square but here… it was just sort of hanging there in the air above the rubble pile. It was almost as if the demons had piled up all this garbage to reach the portal.

Anyway, I couldn't stare at it for more than a second because more guys were coming in behind me. I kept slipping and sliding down the rubble some twenty-thirty feet or so until we reached the cobblestone pavement.

The buildings had an "old world" flavor to them and, looking along the street, about every third one seemed to be in ruins, collapsed and spilling into the street. The sky stretching out to the horizon was orange even with the glasses on but kind of muted.

Ordway led the squad onto the street and we moved off to the right.

Another squad coming in behind us assembled on the street and moved off toward the left. We would clear the way in one direction and they would make another path for the next troops.

Huff pointed the butt end of his weapon toward the scene. "Shit! Looks like this place is falling apart!"

"At least the streets seem to be clear." Wainwright grinned. "Relatively."

"Yeah, but for what?" I nodded along the street. "I don't see a car anywhere."

The Lieutenant raised a hand. "Keep the chatter down, boys."

We zipped it and fell into step behind the Sarge, moving along the street. The buildings on each side showed no signs of life but many of the windows had curtains in them. Maybe the occupants had vacated what appeared to be a war zone or they were just hunkered down low, hoping it would blow past them soon.

We continued toward a bend in the road, spreading out a little to cover both sides, ready for an attack from any quarter. And we had to keep looking up as well in case there were snipers on the rooftops, though it was hard to imagine anyone up there to drop rocks on us.

Just around the corner, a demon stepped out of a doorway. The fellow stood about five feet high and had both arms extended in front of him, both his hands twisting back and forth in a slow wave.

Ferguson had his weapon up first and fired. The demon went down.

Private Huff grinned. "Hot dang! It worked!"

Ferguson patted his rifle. "Smooth as silk."

"All right, men," Ordway cut the celebrations short, "let's keep moving."

Sarge was walking beside the Lieutenant and they turned left at the first intersection, the rest of us a step or two behind. After a dozen feet, the Lieutenant stopped. I craned to see around everyone and saw it was a dead-end. What appeared to be a turn in the street was a blind. It didn't go anywhere.

Ordway shook his head. "What kind of… Okay, back to the main street."

He motioned us back. We turned around but before we could move a group of demons stepped into our path.

Vaudelet swore, "Where the hell did they come from?" as we raised our weapons.

Before the demons could mount any sort of attack, our fire dispersed them. There were no shots fired at us and no enemy dead, but they had been run off.

"Well done, men!" The Lieutenant moved back toward the main street while Sarge looked around at the squad.

"Anyone hurt?" He nodded. "Okay. Let's reassemble, men."

Ordway motioned us forward. "Let's get out of this death trap and back onto the open street." He led the short distance back to the street, turning left to continue moving in the direction we needed to get, toward Satan's palace.

The street bent a little to the left and we tensed as the next section of road was revealed to us but there was nothing there but rubble from a collapsed building off to the right. At the end of the block, it seemed the street ended at a crossing street. We clamored over the spill and reached the cleared pavement beyond.

Other than the sound of us moving daintily along the street, I couldn't hear a sound coming from anywhere. It was like walking through a ghost-town and was beginning to give me the creeps.

Then we heard gunfire in the distance. Apparently the other squad who had come in after us somewhere off toward our left had encountered some resistance. The sound helped settle my nerves. Like Sarge said, it was "same ol' same ol'" and nothing to worry about.

Presently, the Lieutenant stopped in the street. He and Sarge were looking at another street coming in from the left.

When I got close enough I could see that it went down a ways and seemed to turn to the right. The turn looked a little more definite than the last but you couldn't tell with this place, it seemed.

While we were all standing there, Ordway turned to Sarge. "Sergeant, send a couple of men to see if that's another dead end."

"Chou… Kowalski… go check it out."

The two guys nodded and charged down the side street and disappeared around the corner. A moment later, they ran back to the group.

Chou saluted the Lieutenant but spoke to Sergeant Miller. "It keeps going, Sergeant. It goes some distance and turns again."

Sarge looked at the Lieutenant.

He nodded. "Good enough. Let's head out."

Sarge led us down the street, the Lieutenant a step behind, examining the buildings along the way.

"Watch for any signs of a trap, boys." He nodded toward the structures lining the street. There did not appear to be as much damage here as to the ones we had seen on the wider street. It could have meant what the Lieutenant suspected: a trap.

Sarge stopped before the next turn for us to get closer, then signaled Vaudelet and me ahead. We went around the corner and stopped.

"Shit!" Vaudelet raised a hand in disgust.

Ordway came up beside us. "Damn!"

The street was another dead-end.

Sarge overrode the groans and signaled for all of us to reverse course and get back to the main street. "C'mon fellows, let's get out of here."

We turned back but drew up short. From out of nowhere, a group of demons appeared around the corner from where we had come. These guys were ready when they rounded the corner and opened fire.

Ordway could only say, "Damn!!"

We dodged the flying rocks and fell back, firing as we went. One of the stones – about the size of a baseball, hit my shoulder. It might not have done as much damage as any real ordnance but I can tell you it hurt. Anything traveling ninety miles an hour or better would certainly do some damage if it hit the right spot.

We kept moving backward. And firing.

Several of the demons had fallen and it looked like we were about to win the skirmish when another demon, completely different – and larger – stepped into view. This guy must have been at least seven foot tall and the rock he was swinging looked bigger than I wanted to deal with.

Huff was beside me and I heard him say to no one in particular, "Look at the size of that guy! Has he been dipping into the steroids or what?"

But he didn't aim the rock at us. It went over our heads. At first I thought the guy just had a bad aim and kept firing at him to prevent him reloading. Then the wall at the back of the alley crumbled from the blow. The stones and bricks came cascading down and we scooted out of the way.

Pressed between the falling rubble and the attacking demons we were in a tight bunch and I was glad they did not press the attack. Instead, the demons took off. We pursued them around the corner, firing until they disappeared around the farther corner and back onto the main street.

Once the way was clear, we went back to rejoin the group before proceeding. A couple of guys were standing by the corner but Sarge was further back toward the dead-end.

"Give me a hand here." He signaled for us. The guys closest began removing rubble. It looked like one of our guys had gotten buried by the falling wall and, looking around, I was afraid it was the Lieutenant.

Sergeant Miller and the guys had most of the debris off as we gathered around. He looked up grimly. "Our first casualty."

"He's dead?" Huff edge in for a better view.

The Sarge simply looked at the Lieutenant's body and shook his head.

Gingerly removing the helmet from the body, Wainwright looked it over. It was pretty busted up after a ton of rubble had fallen on it. "This thing's worthless now. How are we going to get in touch with headquarters?" He handed it to Sarge.

After a moment, he tossed it aside. "Looks like we are on our own, boys. But that's not going to be a problem. Like the General said, we should not even need to contact anyone. We keep our helmets on."

Ferguson fretted. "But what if we run into something unexpected?"

"We have our orders, soldier. We keep moving and reach the objective." He stood up. "Now, let's get back to the main street. We'll have to send someone back for the Lieutenant later."

We were pretty quiet after that but you could tell that every one was just itching to make the demons pay for our casualty.

Back on the main street, none of the demons were in evidence. Sergeant Miller stared along the street, one way and then the other, then shook his head. "We're not going to keep stumbling blind around here. We need some reconnaissance." He pointed my direction. "Patterson… Wainwright… get to the roof of this building and find us a street that doesn't dead-end on us."

We looked at the building indicated. Most of the buildings were of three floors, some of two. The one he picked was four floors and looked to be the best vantage point in the area.

I saluted. "Yes, sir!" Then I motioned for Wainwright to follow.

Opening the door, I poked my head in quickly and withdrew it. I nodded at Wainwright. "Nothing moving."

I opened the door and we both dashed in, flattening ourselves on either wall of the entryway. Wainwright signaled ahead, indicating a stairway. I nodded.

Opening that door, he also did the quick peek before we entered the stairwell. Weapons pointing upward, we began the slow climb, glancing around to make certain no one approached from either up or down.

At the first floor landing, we switched positions and I took point to go up the next stretch of stairs.

Before I had taken two steps, the door opened. Turning quickly, I saw the demon stop, making a squeaking noise and back away, his two arms extended with his hands making the same slow wave that our first encounter had been doing. After backing a couple of steps, he turned and fled into one of the rooms.

Wainwright lowered his weapon and turned to me. "Now, that was a little weird, wasn't it?"

"Yeah. What do you make of it?"

"I don't know."

I shrugged and get back to climbing the stairs. At the next landing, we switched places again, and Wainwright led us up the last flight.

Standing on each side of the door to the top floor, we both stopped to catch our breaths. After a few moments, he nodded to me and I nodded back, taking ahold of the knob.

We burst out into the corridor and startled a pair of demons coming our way. They appeared to be male and female – don't ask me how I determined that, it's just how it seemed – but before we could aim our weapons, the guy dropped what he was carrying and they both fled down the corridor, disappearing into a room a couple of doors down.

Wainwright looked at me and shook his head. "You know, I really don't think all these guys are out to kill us."

"Doesn't look like it. But where's the roof access?"

We went along the corridor, finding all the doors looked the same. But at the far end was a small alcove with a ladder bolted to the wall.

Wainwright took up a guarding position while I slung my rifle and climbed. At the top was a small square door that lifted easily. Bracing myself against the frame, I unslung the weapon and pushed on the access panel with my head.

Looking first one way and then the other, I saw no signs of any demons and eased up another couple of steps to be able to look around the panel. The roof was empty. I moved upward.

A moment later, as I held the panel open, Wainwright joined me on the flat roof.

After getting our bearings we approached the parapet edge just as gunfire erupted from below.

A group of the larger demons had come around the corner ahead and were drawing fire. In front of them were some of the smaller demons. Some were slinging rocks but several of the guys seemed to be trying to get away but were prevented by the larger fellows behind them.

We took aim on the bigger guys and assisted our guys on the ground. Four of the six larger guys hit the pavement before the rest of the group turned and ran.

Down below, Sergeant Miller looked up and saluted us.

We ran over to the other parapet wall and looked over the street patterns.

I shook my head. "Damn! They sure love dead-ends here, don't they?" In the distance, I could make out a very large structure. "That thing has to be the place we're headed."

"Yeah, and that looks like a big street heading right for it. Now, how do we get there?"

He pointed. "That looks like the way out of here." I followed his finger. "Looks like we should go down that street and turn there. It looks like that street takes us right to that big street."

"Sure looks like it." I nodded and we turned and headed back for the ladder. "What do you make of those demons we encountered?"

He shrugged. "I'd say it looks like the General was wrong. There appear to be some demons who are non-combatants. Both those we encountered in the building and those guys in front of the big monsters on the ground."

"You noticed that too?"

He nodded. "How could you miss it? It looked like they were being used as shields, nothing else."

"So, you gonna tell him or am I?"

"Knock yourself out."

We got back to the ladder and he held the door open for me.

"Thanks." I grinned. "I hope the return trip is as uneventful.

"Yeah. Good luck on that. The way this place works…"

CHAPTER FIVE

Before we reached the bottom floor, we could hear more firing. We raced downward and burst out onto the street with our weapons at the ready. The street in front of the building was quiet. Again, it was the other squad off to our left coming under attack.

Relieved, we ran to rejoin the others.

Wainwright reported. "Sarge, it looks like the cross street that's coming up will lead us into the heart of the city."

Then I added, "It goes for a distance and then a right turn should take us onto that large street running straight through the city toward the palace."

"Good work, men." He turned to give orders but was interrupted by Wainwright.

"And, sir, we ran into a couple of them in the building and it seemed they were non-combatants."

Sarge glared. "And you didn't shoot them? The General said there are no non-combatants. They might give away our position. Next time, I expect you to follow orders." He turned to the others, motioning along the street. "Okay, fellas, let's move out. And be alert." He stared at the two of us as he said that last part.

We moved off. Ferguson moved over between us. He lowered his voice. "Are you sure they were non-combatants?"

"That's how it looked to me." Wainwright nodded. "They seemed to be carrying groceries rather than weapons. They ran in terror when they saw us."

"Let's spread out a little, men," Sarge called over his shoulder. "Let's not make it too easy for them."

So we spread out.

We proceeded cautiously along the avenue, our gaze roving over the street and the buildings. Since Wainwright and I were bringing up the rear, we also had to keep turning to make sure there was no danger approaching from the rear.

Stopping at the corner of the larger crossing road, Sarge sent Garcia and Kowalski to scout out the roadway to the left. They took up positions on both sides of the road and advanced forward a little.

When no sounds of battle came, we all rounded the turn and continued in the new direction with the Sarge signaling for us all the spread out again.

Since this road was wider, we could spread out a little more. Everything was quiet but as the fellows ahead passed a side street and then another, tensions rose. But when nothing happened they eased off until the next one came.

We passed the first set and saw the one on Wainwright's side was obviously a dead-end. The one on my side might pose a problem, I thought. It definitely turned and continued.

The forward pair of our squad was approaching yet another set of alleyways when the action picked up again. I had just turned around to check the rear again when I saw demons coming around from the street we had come from.

I was just about to give a warning call when someone up front did. I turned to see demons pouring out of small alleys both left and right ahead.

Sarge turned to give some order when he saw to guys coming around the corner behind us. "Get to cover!"

Everyone scrambled off the main roadway, disappearing into the available alleyways. The closest to me was the one we had just passed. I dove for it and so did Wainwright. He had seen the one on his side was nothing more than a small alcove.

Looking back, I saw several of the demons turn into the alley behind us. Ahead it bent to the right and we hoofed it.

"I hope it doesn't dead-end. How are we going to shake these guys?"

Wainwright ran to the next turn, to the left, with me right on his heels. Just ahead was a road that crossed ours.

"Maybe we can shake 'em here."

I glanced back and saw no demons in pursuit. "They're not here yet."

We passed through the intersection and the street bent to the right. Before we lost our view of the intersection, I looked back again and still saw none of our pursuers.

"I think we made it!"

Wainwright nodded. "That may buy us a minute. They'll have to figure out which way we went."

Another turn approached. We cut to the left and I glanced back again.

"Damn! They're still coming. It doesn't look like they were fooled."

"What the hell!?"

"Exactly. Let's turn here."

Another smaller alleyway presented itself and we turned down it, dashing for the first turn to see if we could lose these guys. A quick couple of turns later we slammed on the brakes. It was another dead-end with a door on either side.

"Damn! What is it with these people?" I ran to the door on the right while he tried the one on the left. Both doors opened.

I turned to motion to him but he was already going through the other door.

"Come on!" he yelled.

The sound of approaching footsteps told me I'd better move quick. I dashed across the small alley and into the open door. After getting inside, I swiveled and turned what seemed to be the locking bolt. Feeling something on the back of my head, I jerked around to see Wainwright shutting off his helmet. Panicked, I glanced upward and could not see the little red LED.

"Hey! What in hell are you doing?" I could not for the life of me figure out how they had gotten to Wainwright while his helmet was on but I was pretty scared there for a moment. As I reached up to turn it back on, he grabbed my hand and signaled me to silence.

Outside, the sounds of the dozen demons chasing us got close. One of them tried the door we hid behind but, though the knob rattled a bit, it remained locked.

Since the other door opened, the demons went the other direction. We could hear the door open and the running sounds disappeared as it closed.

I let out the breath I had been holding.

"That was a little close."

"Yeah," I agreed, a little hot, "but why did you turn off my headset? I'm open to attack, now."

He shook his head. "These guys knew which way we went far too quickly. I figured if it wasn't from reading our minds, it was from reading these gismos. Either way, it wouldn't hurt to lose them."

"Well, I'm glad to say it worked. But you could have told me sooner. I thought you were under demon mind-control."

"Sorry." He shrugged. "But I just thought of it."

"Still…" Unable to think of anything else, I shrugged too. Then we looked around the room in which we were hiding. A stack of boxes were leaning against a wall. I looked in an open box on top and pulled out what appeared to be a book. Wainwright looked over my shoulder.

It looked like a normal book as far as I could see. I flipped through it. Some form of printed text but a volume without pictures. After a quick flip, I dropped it back it the box. "Books, huh? Who thought these guys would be interested in reading?"

"So, we're either in a bookstore or a library. Let's look around." He cocked his head to a side.

Weapons at the ready we moved slowly along the long dimly lit hallway.

After only about twenty yards the small corridor let out onto a much larger room and, though dim, the ranks of books could easily be seen.

"It's a library."

I nodded. The ranks of shelving were separated a little wider than I recalled our libraries were but the average demon appeared to be a little broader than the average human. Still, the similarity with libraries on Earth made the identity of this building rather easy.

Ahead was an area that was a little less dim from the general stack area and we slowed as we approached, crouching, weapons at the ready.

The ranks of shelves ended at a larger circular seating area where tables and chairs lay empty. Overhead, the ceiling was open to the roof two floors above and a circuit of skylights let in light from outside.

Nodding, Wainwright led the way up the stair, crouched, weapons up, ready for anything. Our progress slowed as we neared the top and could see the floor plan above was even more wide open than below.

There were shelves on the upper level but they were spread out further and better lit up than the lower level due to the large number of skylights scattered throughout the ceiling over the collection of books.

We stopped near the top. The stairs debouched at what appeared to be the front entrance to the building and it was entirely made of glass. Any casual passerby would have a pretty good look at our movements.

An open section had chairs and tables set up like the floor below and the adjacent section had a few desks. Not much good to be had there. One area seemed to have racks of magazines and newspapers. They stood on the floor to a height of about four feet.

I tapped his shoulder and nodded in the direction of these racks. He nodded. Keeping low, we double-timed it to the racks and ducked down behind the first.

Breathing heavily, we squatted there a minute glancing around the corner of the rack to see if there was any movement outside. Everything was quiet. It was difficult to keep reminding myself that this was a war zone. It would have been more convincing if there were signs of an attack going on anywhere.

I wiped the sweat from my forehead and turned to say something to Wainwright when a demon came around the corner.

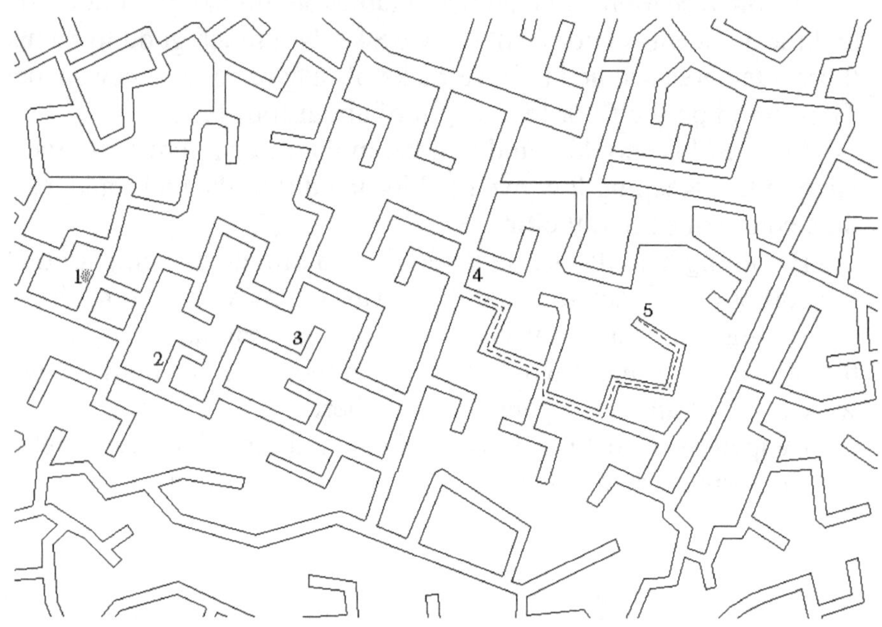

DETAIL OF THE EARLY ACTIONS

1 – insertion point; 2 – first attack by the demons;
3 – second attack where the Lieutenant was killed;
4 – attack of demons from multiple vectors;
5 – path Erik and Bennett took in flight

CHAPTER SIX

It was a bit of a shock. He was as close to me as I am from you at the moment. When he extended his arms in that same funny gesture, with his hands doing the slow wave, he almost touched me. I jumped back and we both raised our weapons but he just continued his little dance and backed up a step or two. I was too stunned to speak.

"Hold it right there, fella. What are you doing here?"

It spoke. "Gentlemen, I work here. I should ask what you're doing here."

My rifle was steady on him. I answered, "We're trying to get away from those demons who were tracking us." I stared closer at him. "Wait. You're not a combatant, are you?"

The demon nodded. "That's correct. As to getting away from the demons tracking you, every one of us has been able to keep track of your whereabouts.

Wainwright chuckled dryly. "Let me guess… the headsets, right?"

The demon gave his version of a shrug, I suppose. "I do not know what it was but all of you have been putting out homing signals since you arrived."

"Damn!"

I lowered my weapon. "We were told that there were no non-combatants but…"

The demon sighed and his head lowered a little. "Sadly, you have learned it a bit late. Hasnardan tried to tell you on your arrival but someone killed him."

Wainwright lowered his weapon as well. "That was a friend of yours?"

"Yes. My name is Grshluk and I have been the head librarian here for many years and," he waved an arm around, "this magnificent collection used to get more attention. But lately we have not even been afforded the power to turn on the lights. I fear the collection and all this knowledge may be lost."

The fate of the demons' library may have been high on his priority list but I don't think it ranked anywhere on my top hundred things-to-do list.

Wainwright asked, "So, this friend… er, late friend of yours… he worked at the library too?"

"No. This has nothing to do with the library. It concerns your invasion. He was working to help you as many of us are." He grimaced. "Is there any way you can get your people to stop killing the ones of us who are trying to help you?"

He shook his head. "I'm sorry but our leaders do not understand that there might be friendlies in this dimension. They assumed everyone here was an enemy and ordered us to shoot anything on sight."

Grshluk looked a bit relieved. "Then, I am pleased you were a little slow in following your orders."

I answered. "It's not so much that, but I've…," I glanced at my partner, "we've both seen enough to convince us that the orders, as given, were wrong."

"Then I thank you for your capacity for intelligence."

I grunted. Was that some sort of inter-dimensional joking reference to the ubiquitous "military intelligence"? Who knows, perhaps it was an oxymoron in Hell as well.

The demon was continuing, "Yes, there are many of us opposed – well fewer than there once was – opposed to the plans of Klakmonidos."

I held up a hand. "Hold on! Who's this Klak character you're bringing up?"

He blinked at me as if I had yodeled or something. "He's the tyrant who rules over us, of course. He's the one who… Oh, yes, I suppose you people know him as Satan. Is that what you call him?"

My partner nodded. "Yeah. You can say that again."

I continued. "Okay. It's obvious you're not a friend of his but how did this come about? Why doesn't someone overthrow the guy? If enough of you don't like what he's doing…"

"You make it sound so simple. But he has been in charge for a long time and I think there are as many with him as those who oppose him. It might have been possible in his father's time."

"Wait!" Wainwright held up a hand. "You mean Satan had a father?"

The demon chuckled and stared as if my buddy was now the idiot child. "What? Doesn't everyone? Oh, yes, indeed. His father ruled, and his grandfather before that."

"This is crazy! Satan first interacted with humans in the Garden of Eden. That would have been…" He glanced at me for support but this was well outside my bailiwick. "I don't know… Something like six thousand years ago!"

"That would have been the grandfather, I suppose. He was the first who found a way into the other realm, your world. The power he gained thereby led to him becoming the lord of this realm. As he gained support and power, he began to grow in size as well."

"Before that," I said, "he looked just like the rest of you?"

He nodded. "As he gained power, it seemed to transform him. Most of his followers, you will have noticed, are larger than the majority of the population."

"And I had thought it was some sort of mutational thing or that there were several different species of demons."

"It is representative of the change that comes over the person. After the grandfather ruled many years, his son took over and continued the same type of invasive interference in your world. Then Klakmonidos came along and he could not be satisfied with that sort of thing. He has tried to find ways to make the inter-dimensional barrier more porous. And with his increasing powers, he keeps increasing in size."

"So how old is this guy, this Klak fellow, this Satan?" Wainwright asked.

"Many centuries, I am sure. But I would have to check the relevant texts to give you a precise date."

"Don't bother." I waved my rifle toward the door. "This is all very interesting, I am sure, but we have an invasion to get back to." With a nod to Wainwright, I turned to go.

The demon wailed. "That is what Hasnardan was trying to warn you about."

"Warn us?" My departure was brought up short. I glanced at Wainwright.

"Yes. You are walking into a trap."

"Yes," Wainwright glanced at me, "we're sure they have something in mind to –"

"No, no, you do not understand. There is a trap, yes, but this whole episode is a trap. Klakmonidos thinks he can make a permanent doorway into your world by creating a large enough bloodbath at one time."

My buddy stared at me and seemed at a loss for words, for once. "And how do you know about his plans?" I asked.

"Oh, he has made no secret of them. These demons you have encountered… they meet in small groups and attempt to force you to hold up in dead-end streets, correct? They do not come after you in any great force." He saw our nods. "They are waiting for your leaders to send more troops."

We exchanged glances again.

"Yeah. And what's the plan?" Wainwright asked.

"When enough of your troops have entered this realm, all his forces will fall back along the broad avenue leading to his citadel."

"Yeah, we saw that street." I nodded in agreement. "I wondered why it didn't look like anything else around here."

"Yes, it was a recent construction. He had many buildings torn down to create it. And when enough of your people are all gathered on that causeway, he will unleash his big weapon."

I didn't stammer. "And what would that be?"

But Grshluk only shrugged. "That, I do not know for certain. Although he has publicized his plans widely among us – probably to keep a lot of us out of the way – he has not shared exactly what his weapon is. I only know that he is satisfied it will accomplish his aims. On that, he gloats often."

Again it seemed things were going pear-shaped. The mission we were on – which was questionable to begin with – was now shown to be playing right into Satan's hands. Now, I ask you, what else is new?

So I said, "What do we do now? We have to get the word back to 'Ironguts' before he sends the next wave through."

"Yeah, but how can we get through the streets safely? Even without the helmet being on, I am sure us running through the streets would draw more than a couple of demons in chase."

"We outran them once," I reminded him. "We could probably get all the way back to the opening even with them on our tails. And I'm sure they've established HQ on this side of the opening by now."

"Yeah, but do you remember the way back? We've taken so many turns," he shook his head, "that I think we'd get even further lost trying to backtrack."

"I got that one covered." I chuckled. After so many video games with mazes and such, I had a knack for remembering which way I had come and which direction I was headed. Call it some sixth-sense, but I always had a built-in compass and never got lost. But we didn't get to test it out that day.

"Come with me." Grshluk motioned us across the lobby. "There is another way you may not have thought of."

We exchanged shrugs and followed.

Before we left the lobby area, the demon said, "It would also be most helpful if I knew your names as well. Saying 'hey' and 'you there' will become very trying after a time, you know."

"My apologies!" I laughed. "I'm Patterson and this ugly fellow here is…"

"Speak for yourself!"

"… is my good buddy, Wainwright."

"Patterson. Wainwright. Very difficult and unusual names, but I shall try to keep them straight."

Wainwright looked at me and rolled his eyes.

Grshluk stopped at a doorway. "We must go up to the roof." He opened the door and started up the stairs. We followed.

It was far more a casual ascent than we had experienced in the apartment building earlier. First, Grshluk didn't seem to be in any hurry – if he was even capable of such – and we did not have to cover each other at every flight.

We arrived on the roof after only two flights of stairs. The sky was as bright as it had been when we arrived.

"I don't see the sun here at all. Is it always this same orange overcast?"

Grshluk looked at me. "Sun? What are you talking about?"

"Don't you have day and night?" Wainwright asked. "When does it get dark here?"

"Dark?" He looked from one of us to the other. "Oh! Like on your world. No, we have nothing like that here." He waved a small hand toward the sky. "It is always just as you see it now."

"An insomniac's dream world," Wainwright grinned.

I grunted. "More like his nightmare, I should think. At least there should be some darker period to induce sleep. What do y'all do about sleeping? Are there set times or don't y'all bother with that?"

He shrugged. "We have our periods of hibernation when we tire and are occupied when we are awake. It is nothing like the standardized periods on your world."

"And how long are you usually awake at one time?"

He shrugged. "Without a comparable temporal referent, I cannot think of a duration that would mean anything."

I tried again. "Since you met us it has been about a quarter-of-an-hour, our time. How many of those periods are you normally awake?"

"Let me think…"

Wainwright was beginning to fidget a little. And I had been the one to remind him earlier that we had an invasion to get back to. I gave him a look and said, "It doesn't really matter, we…"

"I would say about two hundred of those periods would be my normal wakeful period."

I did the math quickly. "Fifty hours!?"

He shrugged. "It differs from one of us to another. Many tell me I sleep too much and too often. They call me slothful."

"Doesn't sound very slothful to me." I nodded toward Wainwright. "But we better get back to the business at hand. We want to try to save our guys from that big trap Satan has planned."

"Right." Wainwright nodded. "So what's your plan to getting us back to the inter-dimensional portal?"

He walked across the roof toward the direction we came. "There is the portal."

In the distance, over the maze of assorted rooftops, was the whiter glow from Saint Peter's Square shining into hell. From here you could see a few walkways between buildings at the roof level. Why hadn't we noticed those before?

"I believe you can traverse most of the distance safely along the upper walkways. They are stabilized and virtually invisible from the ground. You could cross over a crowd of demons and they would not even know you are there." He shrugged. "Some of the narrower passageways do not have such contrivance but I suppose you could jump across?" He saw Wainwright nod.

"But why are they invisible from below?" I asked. "What's the purpose in that?"

"Years ago we used to have fireworks displays and many complained they could not see them properly because of the walkways. So they made them invisible."

Grinning, Wainwright said, "I'd like to know how they do that."

"Later, Tiger, let's get moving." With each of us getting interested in one aspect or another of this world we could probably spend a week asking questions. But we had really better get back to work or things might go south before we got a chance to be the heroes.

Wainwright returned to mapping out a strategy with the walkways. "There's a couple of places I can't see real good," he pointed, "like the area behind that building…" It looked sort of like the apartment building we had been on top of earlier. "…but I think the path looks fairly simple."

"Great!" I turned to Grshluk. "And how many do you say are working in your underground movement to fight Satan… Klakmonidos?"

"Many hundreds, I should think."

"Good. Now how can we coordinate your guys with our guys?"

He thought a moment. "It might be best if one of you came with me. It might save hours of explanation."

"Be my guest." Wainwright motioned to me. "I'll take the hard job of trying to convince 'Ironguts' of what's really going on."

I nodded. "Okay. But how can we stay in contact?"

"If I might," Grshluk looked at each of us, "I could send some friends who can help coordinate with the larger group of rebels. They will ask for you specifically, Wainwright, so do not have your friends shoot them on sight."

"Got it!" He climbed up on the wall. "Good luck to you. Oh, and Eric, if you could find out how they do those invisible bridges…"

"Certainly, pal. Now get going!"

We watched him make it across the first walkway and hop off on the next roof over. He looked back and waved, then dropped out of sight onto another walkway.

I turned to Grshluk. "Okay. Where the walkways we have to take?"

He shook his head. "No, the walkways would take far too long to get where we need to go. We shall have to go down to the subway."

"You've got a subway here?" I turned to see Bennett running across another roof. "Why couldn't he have used it?"

"Well, there's a little problem with that…"

CHAPTER SEVEN

We descended back to the lobby and kept going. The first level down must have been the level we had entered the library from, through the back door, but we kept going down. There were two other floors along the descent but we did not stop until we reached the bottom of the stair.

There was no door and very little light.

"I can't see anything."

"Sorry," Grshluk said, "but with the power situation being what it is, we have to rely on the back-ups and they do not emit much light. Sorry."

"Hopefully, my eyes will adjust soon." I waited and waited but it did not improve much.

"Perhaps if you removed those goggles…"

Oops! I reached up and pulled them off. Suddenly, I could see. Not perfectly, it was still dim as shadow, but I could see the subway station before me. "That's better. But with the power being out, I imagine the trains aren't running either, are they? That's the problem you were talking about?"

"Precisely."

"So why are we down here then?"

"This is the fastest way out of town. With most of the streets above being guarded by the followers of Klakmonidos, this is the safest course."

"I see." I nodded and glanced both ways along the empty tracks. "Okay, which way leads where?"

Grshluk pointed left. "That direction leads to the station before the Northern Market. I should say 'led to' as that station was demolished when Klakmonidos created the causeway." Motioning to the right, "This way leads us out of the town and into the countryside." He began moving along the tunnel. "It is some distance out of town but this is actually straighter and faster than the surface."

I shouldered my weapon and grunted. "Yeah, uh-huh. Whatever." I am not what you would call afraid-of-the-dark nor am I exactly a claustrophobe, but when the two are combined it does tend to make me a little uneasy. Double-timing, I caught up to the demon and walked abreast of him.

"So, can you tell me anything about the interactions of your world with Earth? I mean, if you know of any." My interest was not particularly stringent but I thought talking might distract my unease.

"Oh, where to start." Grshluk sighed. "As I said, the first encounter came in the time of Bekramta – Klamonidos' grandfather – although I am not privileged to know anything of the details of the event. From what I gather, the fellow was dabbling in something that he should not have." He waved a hand. "Anyway, contact was made and the fellow apparently discovered that he gained sustenance from the terror he created." He shook his head. "I am not certain how he discovered this but it has since been found out that many of us are not capable of deriving energy from such an action."

"Are you saying some of you demons are not really demons?"

He nodded. "Apparently so. Some genetic quirk, I suppose. Only about ten to fifteen percent of the population seems capable of such. They are the ones who tend to a larger size than the rest of us."

I grunted. "As usual, it seems our intelligence gathering has been a little spotty." There was a noise from ahead that distracted me.

"That may not have been an oversight on your people. I believe Klakmonidos was trying to create the impression that we were all a danger to you. Otherwise the large invading force he required would not have been forthcoming. It seems…"

The sounds ahead caused me to interrupt him. "Grshluk, what is that up ahead? It sounds like water. Is this tunnel leaking?" Darkness, and claustrophobia, and a flashflood were the trifecta to my mind. I stopped.

He continued forward. "No, not any more, I should think."

"Not any more?!"

"No, I…" He noticed I was no longer beside him and stopped, turning. "Is there a problem?"

"When were you going to tell me about this water? How deep is it?"

"I really did not see it as a problem. It is no more than a few feet deep and it has been at the low point of the tunnel for over a decade I should think."

Hesitantly, I moved forward. "So, it's nothing new? Not currently leaking?"

A casual gesture showed his lack of concern. "Of course not. Had there been any danger I most certainly would have mentioned it. That along with the kasidnas."

"What?!" I stopped again. "What are these kassidens?"

"Kasidnas." He glanced around abstractedly. "I suppose you would call them semi-amphibious rodents…"

"Rats!?" I was trying to figure what was one more than a trifecta – a quadrifecta? – when he laughed.

"Oh, no, not rats, assuredly." He chuckled for another moment while my apprehension began to subside. "No, the kasidnas are much larger than a simple rat."

"Oh, brother!"

Starting forward again, he motioned me to continue. "As long as we are moving they should not present any problem. They are skitterish creatures and will usually only attack something that is not moving."

"'Usually'?"

"Well, yes, of course." He hummed a non-descript tune while we moved along the tunnel. After a bit, he added, "Unless, of course, they have not eaten in some time. They might throw caution to the wind in that case." He shrugged. "Still with two of us passing through, I doubt we shall have any trouble."

Glancing around ahead, I muttered, "I hope you're right."

The sounds of the water grew closer.

"As do I, my friend. As do I."

Great, I thought, as my boot splashed in a shallow puddle. "Perhaps we should walk a little faster."

"By all means."

Our pace increased until the depth began to impede our acceleration. The water rose above my knees, halfway up my thighs, and then to my waist. My breath grew a little ragged but my attention was completely focused on pushing forward. Until something brushed against my leg.

"What the…?!" Looking at the surface of the water it seemed as if shapes were moving beside me… around me… Another brushed against my butt. I glared at the demon. "Tell me, is this going to get any deeper?"

His head shook in short jerks. "No, this is as deep as it gets but it does continue at this depth for a time."

"Then I say we run." And with that, I pushed forward against the stagnant water just as hard as I could. Behind me, I could hear his pace increase as well.

Now I have run in marathons before and, though they are no picnic, they were a Sunday stroll next to trying to run almost chest deep in a think soup. Ahead was the same gray as we had been moving through since we entered the tunnel. The sensation was similar to crazy dreams I've had about running away from monsters… though here I was running beside one.

A dim shape hovered ahead on my right. "What's that?" was about all I could pant out as I continued concentrating on pushing forward.

"That would appear to be the Omagoloon Station."

"A loading platform, you mean?"

"Yes."

I angled to the side and almost tripped over some steps leading up to the waiting platform. My hands splashed and found the upper steps and halted my forward pitch as my soggy feet labored up the rough steps.

The solid stone platform was completely dry and I collapsed onto the surface, rolling onto my back, gasping huge gulps of air. At some point, Grshluk joined me but I could not swear to how long it was before he arrived.

I would like to have hit the fellow for not giving me proper warning about what was coming but I was too exhausted to do anything about it. As counter-productive as such action might have been it would certainly have felt good, even so.

But I simply lay there, trying to catch my breath, and gather some strength to keep going.

I thought about Bennett waltzing across the rooftops and wished that I had gotten that cush job and let him have this scurrying about in the dark.

Later I found out a bit more of his "cush" job.

CHAPTER EIGHT

Bennett had gone across a couple of roofs and skirted over a pair of streets on their hanging walkways before he dropped to a lower roof out of sight from my position atop the library. Not that I was there to witness it as Grshluk and I had already turned to descend to the subway.

The pathways across the tops of the buildings seemed to be rather straightforward from our earlier vantage point. Of, if only that could at least have turned out better but it seems everything in Hell was… well, simply Hellish!

And I was laying on that platform in the subway wishing I could have been the one to go across the roofs!

We had only run about six blocks – by my reckoning – from our beachhead and the going across the rooftops and the walkways should have been a piece of cake. And it would have been, too, if only there had been walkways where there should have been.

After Bennett had dropped to a lower roof and skirted across its flatness to the next street, he found no more walkways. At least none heading in the right direction. It looked as if he should take one heading further to the east – if the cardinal directions meant anything in Hell – or in the direction of the large causeway we were trying to keep our men away from, he could work his way back to where he wanted to go. At least that's how it looked from his new vantage.

But it Hell, appearances could be so deceiving!

He went across a couple of more rooftops and streets before he ran out of options. He could have dropped down to another lower roof but there seemed no exit from the next level down but what appeared to be a walkway on the next level up. Which would mean he would have to descend to the street and enter an adjacent building and find the way back up to its roof.

Peering over the side, he could see bands of demons skulking around evidently searching for some way to disrupt more troops. He thought of firing down on the group. With his limited fire power, he thought the idea would be suicide.

Walking the perimeter of the roof he was on, he noticed a series of small balconies on the building he wanted. It would be quite a jump so he looked for something else instead. After another circuit of the roof, he decided it was really his only choice.

He backed up some distance to get a running start, strapped his rifle securely across his back and got set. Just as he started his run, a door opened on the roof and several demons poured out and looked to step between him and the jump site.

Adrenalin kicked in and he was able to bolt past the startled group, though one was able to grab at his arm. He jerked a bit to the side to prevent any firm grip and was lucky they did not grab the rifle strap.

Still, he was now a little off his original trajectory.

A moment later his foot hit the top of the small perimeter wall and he was airborne, flailing to adjust his angle to hit the small balcony. It was a little off but he caught the railing as he collided with the brick wall and hung precariously for a moment with the wind knocked out.

Glancing over his shoulder, he saw the pursuing demons at the edge of the other roof peering over at him, and it looked as if they were preparing to fire. Without waiting to see what they were up to, he pulled himself over the railing and kicked at the curtained glass door, keeping low and rolling into the room as rocks crashed against the side of the building, some smashing windows, others thudding against the brick wall.

After shaking his head to clear it, he looked up to see a small family at a table, spoons raised halfway to their mouths. Before they could even react, Bennett was back on his feet and racing through the apartment. Through the second room adjacent, he spotted a door.

Pulled it open, he was relieved to see the hallway. What he did not want was to encounter some weird sort of maze with the possibility of pursuit on the way. He heard a scream from behind him but did not wait to investigate.

After glancing both ways, he took off in the direction he thought the stairs should be – as if anything was as it should be in this place – and was relieved again to see his hunch pay off.

When he reached the top of the stairs, he burst through the door into the open air, rifle at the ready. On the opposite roof he saw the group of demons who had assaulted him, swarming back through the door on that roof, going down. Slowly, he eased over toward the edge, peering over to see what lay below.

Leaning out a little over the edge, he saw one demon laying in a heap in the roadway, evidently one tried jumping across but failed. That was probably the source of the scream he had heard. It was one of the smaller fellows and he wondered if the guy had jumped or been pushed. Regardless, he figured the remainder were heading for the ground level to come up the stairs after him.

Turning to the walkway, he proceeded across, looking ahead, trying to determine the best route to the beachhead HQ so he could warn the commander. It seemed the only way to get to his destination was rather circuitous. And with possible bogeys on his tail, he had better slip it into high gear.

He picked up the pace and trotted across the next roof to the next causeway.

CHAPTER NINE

When I had caught my breath a little more, I rolled over on my side and looked at the demon. As tired as I was, I still had a wealth of questions. "So, exactly what is it that attracts the demons to Earth?"

He sighed and shook his head. "Power, I'm afraid." His eyes drifted upward though there was nothing to be seen in the dim shadows overhead. "There is not much of what you would call a history of the recent times. Ever since Klakmanidos' grandfather found a way to cross over into your realm our society has dwindled. No longer are there enterprising young minds trying to better our situation... All energies have gone toward the effort to encroach further and further into the other world.

"Most of the decent sorts of us have been sacrificed, killed off to fuel this thirst for the power they have found in this other realm. The ones found to be capable of crossing the divide become changed physically, mutated."

"You're talking about those larger brutes?"

He nodded. "I do not know if the change is brought on by the journey to the other realm or if it is the change that manifests the capability. And those lesser ones of us are discarded by whim, it would seem."

I sat up. "You mean they have to use... some form of sacrifice to make the transition?"

"Sadly, yes." Another long sigh escaped. "Klakmanidos discovered that there was something in the stars and such to strengthen the use of blood-letting to facilitate their egress. Either here or on that side as well. Most of the wars in your human history have occurred at opportune moments when the veil was easier to pass through. The greater the blood payment the larger the rift and the more easily they could pass over."

"But what about this latest one? I don't recall anything in our history that equals this portal. Has this sort of rift happened before?"

"No. This is a first." He sat up. "Klakmanidos has been busy for quite a few years in experimentation; trying first one method and then another to force a stable passageway between the worlds."

"So how did he do it?" I got to my feet. "This could be important to learning how to close it again."

Grshluk hung his head. "That I do not know. Not even a hint." He seemed to pause, thinking. "Although…"

"D'ya think of something?"

"It may not mean much but it could possibly emanate from the soul containment facility."

"The what?!"

"The soul containment… I believe you would call it purgatory or some such."

"Wait. I thought hell and purgatory were the same thing."

He shrugged and got back to his feet. "I may have the equivalent terminology confused. From what I gather, 'hell' is what you would call this world of ours, where we live, and 'purgatory' would be the place where the souls are… well, kept prisoner."

I had to think about that real hard for a minute. Sure, I knew that hell was where the bad souls were sent but I did not recall seeing any here. Unless, of course, I thought they had become the demons but that didn't sound right. Ironguts hadn't mentioned anything about hostages being held here but – if the myths were right – there had to be some souls being kept some place around here.

"Okay," I said at last, "so where is this purgatory place? Hopefully not another long tunnel journey ahead."

"Oh, no, no." Grshluk chuckled. "It is outside the city. Quite nearer our current destination than the portal through which you entered this world."

"Okay. No more tunnels, right?"

"Correct. Our exit will be where the tunnel ends."

Squaring my shoulders, I nodded back to the watery channel. "I guess we better get moving again." My slacks had no time to dry out in this humid place and it felt almost more comfortable to be back into the underground river.

Down the few steps and we were off again.

"This is crazy. It reminds me so much of a damned video game."

Grshluk asked, "What's that?"

"This tunnel, you know, it's just like… "

"No, I mean what is, I believe you called it a 'video game'?"

I laughed. "Oh, that's something we play to while away the time back home. You know, shooting up enemies and… uh, well, uh… monsters."

Grshluk snorted. "It seems your people are violent even in your pastimes. 'Game', indeed."

We walked along in silence for a time. I changed the subject. "So, how much further do we have to go in this muck?"

"Not too far. We're over halfway along now."

A short distance ahead, the sounds in the tunnel changed a bit.

"What's that up ahead?" My voice had an echoey quality to it. "To the left."

"That is where the tracks from the citadel converge with this track."

"The citadel. Is that Satan… Klakie's home?"

He nodded. "Yes, it is."

"Do you think we could…"

"I would not advise attempting that tunnel, sir. It was underwater even while this one was still in operation. Klakmonidos had it flooded some time ago." Before I could respond again, he continued, hurriedly. "And I would suggest we try and move a little faster through this area." His pace increased.

"No, don't tell me." My feet sped up as well. "Another wonderful surprise you just forgot to let me in on, huh? What now? Radioactive eels?"

His breath was coming faster as he pushed forward, practically trying to run through the better-than-waist-deep current. "I do not… know what 'radioactive'… means, but… your estimate about… eels is quite astute."

Damn! Guess I'm too smart, huh? The thought was not spoken as the exertion of keeping up with the fellow took all my breath. I was going to ask if the fellows made any discernible sounds but the racket we were making drowned out any possibility of stealth.

"One thing," he shouted between deep breaths, "keep your… legs high… don't want… them to wrap… around… you'll go down."

"Great!" And I joined his high-stepping jog.

Once again, just as with the rodents earlier, I was feeling things moving through the water, brushing up against me. And, yes, they were wrapping themselves around my legs but only one at a time. I kicked higher to keep them from gaining any purchase on both legs at once.

That's when something brushed against the back of my neck.

"Hey!" I swatted and got a palm-full of air. "They're coming at my head!"

"I doubt that," he said without slowing, "that must… be the bats."

"Bats!?"

I did not have the energy to ask him why he didn't mention that little item a little earlier either. Scrunching my head down deep between my shoulders, I continued trying to increase the speed and keep those knees pumping high, high, high!

"Any more… *surprises*… coming?"

All he could manage was shaking his head. I was surprised he could keep up the pace. My fitness was supposed to be peak form but he – a sedentary librarian, supposedly – was setting a pace that was hard for me to maintain.

Of course, he was on his home turf and I was new to the neighborhood.

Still, it was impressive.

Before too much longer, I noticed the water level begin to drop. The traveling got harder as well due to exhaustion but we were coming to the end of the deeper water. By the time it was down to our knees, Grshluk was back to a brisk walk. His breathing sounded labored to me but when he spoke I realized the labored breath was my own. Jeez!

"We are almost… there." He raised an arm and pointed ahead. "Should see… some light… just to the right… soon."

No sooner had he spoken the words than the lighter wall section became apparent. Pulling closer, it appeared to be another loading platform like the last one we had rested on. And I would say we both needed a bit of a rest.

The steps were not obstructed by water, which made them easier to navigate, but the difficulty lay in my tired legs. It was like lifting blocks of concrete up each yard-high step. I almost pitched forward on my face before I reached the top step.

We reached the top and, well, collapsed, of course.

After laying there breathing for a time, I figured we might as well push on before I fell asleep. If we could continue a normal pace for a time, I could rest up while we moved. It would also help keep my muscles from cramping.

I rolled onto my side. "Ready to keep going?"

"I suppose we must." He sighed heavily and lumbered back to his feet. "If we are going to get to help before your people fall into the trap."

"As long as this is taking, I don't know if we are going to be doing any good. The guys may be already on the causeway by now."

He went toward a door at the inside edge of the platform. "Oh, no, they are not that far along yet."

"How can you be sure?"

Turning, he stared at me a moment before opening the door. "Remember, I am in telepathic communication with others in my group."

"Oh, yeah, yeah, that's right. How could I forget?" I went through the door after him wondering how I could even *remember* such a thing. This was all pretty new and unusual to me. "So where are they now?"

"Most of your people have stayed fairly close to the entry point establishing a… some special formation…"

"A beachhead."

"Yes, whatever that means. Since the skirmishers were keeping the small groups pinned down, your commander has seen fit to send in more men… a second… type of group…"

"The second wave."

"Yes, that's it. But they are waiting to reach an optimum strength level before advancing."

As he talked it struck me that we were using seafaring lingo. "Beachhead", "second wave". Terms like that must be very foreign to a place that has no ocean… only infested underground slimy tunnel rivers.

And I was glad to see it behind me.

CHAPTER TEN

While I was busy trying to catch my breath on the second platform, I believe it would have been about the time that Bennett finally arrived back at the entry point although I could have the timing off by a bit.

After leaving the roof finally escaping the demons, he got a couple of buildings away before the guys appeared on the roof behind him. Apparently, he was so close to the entry that they gave up the chase and simply went back inside the building.

Reaching the final building, he went down the stairs and exited on the roadway just in front of the local HQ set up by Captain Anderson.

The Captain was standing in the tented canopy talking on a field-set when Bennett arrived.

Placing his hand over the mouthpiece, the Captain stared at him. "Where did you come from, soldier? What's your unit?" He glanced around the street, both directions. "Where's your unit?"

After saluting, Bennett said, "Sorry to startle you, sir. PFC Wainwright, attached to Lieutenant Ordway's unit. The Lieutenant was killed a couple of streets over and the unit was split up. I've got some intel for the General."

The Captain just stared at him a minute. Then, "Just a second, soldier." He raised the field-set again and said, "Hold your position until further orders. I'll get back to you." He seemed to listen for a moment before adding, "Just hunker down and hold the position. We're preparing to send in reinforcements." He re-seated the phone and turned to Bennett. "Things aren't going too good here, Wainwright, so make it quick. General Strittmeier is about to send in the next wave."

"That's what I need to tell you about, sir. I have learned information that says we are marching into a trap."

"And where'd you get this information?"

With a straight face, Bennett answered, "From one of the enemy captives, sir. I interrogated one."

"That's amazing, Wainwright." The Captain grunted. "So far, no one else has been able to capture a single demon. What's this trap?"

"Well, sir, their orders are to force all our men into places where they have to hold up, dead-ends and such. And when the second wave comes through, they are going to fall back and draw us into a major firestorm. They have some big weapon they're holding in reserve."

The Captain chewed the inside of his cheek for a moment before motioning to him. "Come with me, soldier."

Bennett followed the Captain up and back through the vortex into Saint Peter's Square. Another officer stood nearby engrossed in his clipboard. Anderson stopped before the guy and saluted.

"Major Hopkins, sir. We have finally had some decent intel from on the ground." He motioned to Bennett. "Private Wainwright here is from Ordway's unit. They captured one of the enemy and interrogated the fellow. He claims they are fighting a holding pattern, delaying our advance until we send in more troops." He glanced at Bennett, who nodded. "And after the second wave arrives, they plan on falling back until our troops are in a position for them to unleash some secret weapon."

The Major scowled at Bennett and looked back down at his clipboard. "I see nothing in the intel about any secret weapon." He looked at the Captain. "It seems a rather far-fetched tale. How do we know the intel is worth anything? How do we know this is some dis-information planted to force us to alter the invasion strategy?"

Bennett started, "I'm not sure, sir, but…"

The Captain cut him off. "Sir, this information does explain why our troops are being pinned down wherever they go. The demons aren't overrunning our troops on any front. It does seem like they're waiting for something." He motioned toward the entrance to Hell. "I've been in contact with all the units engaged with the enemy and they all tell the same story. Even where our numbers are reduced, the enemy is not advancing on any front." He shook his head. "It does appear to be some sort of holding action."

The Major cursed and glanced over to where the General was preparing the second wave. "Yes, Captain, I'm afraid this intel does seem to match what we're seeing on the ground no matter how farfetched it sounds. Some of us had thought that it was simply that the demons were new to combat situations." He nodded firmly. "And I'll be damned if I can see any other reason for their tactics. But with the General already set to swagger the mission I don't see any way we can order a withdrawal. And I don't think he wants to hear any sort of drop-kick solution at this point." He turned to Bennett. "And you say you have a captive? Is he being held nearby?"

Shaking his head, Bennett said, "No, sir, he is quite some distance from here. I returned over the roofs but I don't think it would be safe to try and bring him back through the streets."

"Yes, I see. The enemy would obviously strike hard to free one of their own." He paused while a troop of men rushed past. "Gentlemen, looks like the second wave is going in. Extraction of the troops is impossible at this stage and risky. Without the prisoner present for the General to question, I cannot go to him with this matter."

Another troop ran past their discussion and disappeared through the portal.

"Captain Anderson, if this pans out, you will have to report this development to all your units. They need to be ready for the trap when it's sprung. If it's sprung. Send the order out to hold their positions – even if that's all they've been doing – and then we'll go talk to the General. Meanwhile I have to make sure everything is in position for the next wave." He nodded to the Captain and then to Bennett and went back to his clipboard.

Anderson saluted. "Yes, sir. Wainwright, you come with me."

They followed the next unit through the vortex and back down into Hell stopping at the local HQ at the base of the hill of rubble.

"Good work, soldier." Captain Anderson clapped him on the shoulder. "I hope we can circumvent their plans."

Bennett said, "Uh, sir, I was wondering if anyone has reported any friendlies in the area?"

"Friendly demons? Not a word." He stared at Bennett. "Do you know something, Wainwright, or is that a rhetorical question?"

"Well, sir, maybe it's just a hunch, but I think some of the locals we encountered were as anxious to get away from us as any other non-combatant would. My Sergeant said the idea was ridiculous. Still, it had me wondering."

The Captain considered it a moment. "In this realm, soldier, I have found very little that I would not consider ridiculous. I'll check with our units in the field and see if anyone has noticed anything like that. But first of all, we have to coordinate our advance." He turned to another soldier nearby. "Lieutenant Benavides, work with Wainwright here and see if we can circumvent a disaster, okay?" He sighed. "I've got some radio work to do."

CHAPTER ELEVEN

We stepped out of the subway system into the bright orange light of the surface. I had to dig out my goggles again to counteract the damned orange glow and was happy to be able to *see* things again.

Before us were a few small dwellings in a cluster surrounded by fields. It was apparently a farming community although I could not see any farming activity going on presently unless they performed farming entirely different than on Earth.

Turning to look back the way we came, I could see no trace of the city. Trees surrounded the farming enclave and obscured the demon metropolis.

"How far have we come?"

Grshluk shrugged. "I do not know if our measures of distance would mean anything to you."

"All right." I shifted my rifle. "Where to now?"

"This way." He motioned for me to follow as he took off. "There are a few of our resistance cell meeting in a barn and we can coordinate with their help and hopefully avert a disaster befalling us all."

I gazed out across the field as we went, and chuckled. "Wow! Who would have thought… farming in Hell!"

Grshluk snickered. "Yes, weird, huh? I guess though that we do have to eat, just like any other species."

"Sorry, Grshluk, I just meant…"

"No matter. Though there are very few of the opposition left in the city, in this area it is quite the reverse."

"That's good."

As we strode along a path through the closest field, it seemed to me that the crops had gone past their harvest time. The plants looked a lot like wheat but the kernels at the end of the stalk were ragged. Some were fallen to the ground while others were bloated, or moldy, or already sprouting small tendrils.

"Isn't anyone working these fields?"

His voice came over his shoulder. "No, the harvest has passed without any harvesting being done. Most the population was called to the city to construct the massive causeway Klakmonidos demanded. I'm afraid too many of us will starve because of this but he seems to think we are all expendable to his loftier plans."

"Huh. Surely someone would have harvested something."

"Well, there are a few fields that have been harvested but the manpower has been too light to get to all of them. Such as this one."

Once we passed through the field, he angled toward the closest barn.

"Our group is meeting in here."

"So, how many are in this little group you have?"

Stopping at the door, Grshluk said, "Only around fifty in this group, though I doubt if that many are showing up for this meeting. Only eight or so of the leaders will be in attendance today."

"And your group has a plan?"

Stopping with a hand on the knob, Grshluk shook his head. "Not exactly. Hasnardan thought he could warn you earlier, but he was killed."

"Yeah, and I'm really sorry about that. We were told there were no friendlies."

"'Friendlies'? You mentioned that before. What does it mean?"

"You know, natives that might not be trying to kill us."

"I see." He sighed and pushed the door open. "But other than that plan, we had not devised anything else workable. There were too many variables to work with."

I stepped through the door behind him. "Ain't that the truth!"

It took a few moments for my eyes to adjust to the dim interior. And it helped a lot when I remembered to take the goggles off. Several demons were seated around a rather rustic looking table and they looked up as we entered. Several drew back in surprise when they saw me.

One guy with his back to the door started talking before he turned around.

"About time, Grshluk. We've been…" Then he noticed me. "What's this? You brought an alien with you?!"

"Yes," Grshluk said. "I thought we could…"

Then things happened a bit faster than I am used to. At least in a barn setting.

The fellow, whose name turned out to be Voshparlet, jumped to his feet and reached inside his jacket. As his hand appeared with a weapon, Grshluk snatched my rifle from my hands and turned it on the guy.

Voshparlet screamed, "Treason! We are not supposed to…"

He had the weapon raised but Grshluk fired a round into the fellow's head before he could get off a shot.

Everyone else jumped up from their seats, terrified. Before things deteriorated further, I snatched the rifle back from Grshluk.

"What's going on here?" I was glaring at my host.

"I hope he did not have time to warn his people that you were here."

I turned to stare at the corpse, then the others present who were starting to move back to their seats. "Warn *his* people?"

"Yes, didn't I mention we normally communicate telepathically?"

I nodded.

The older fellow present had regained his seat. "Grshluk, did you already suspect Voshparlet?"

Grshluk shrugged. "Burevost… friends…We all suspected someone. I thought the sudden appearance of a human might reveal the traitor in our midst. It is not that I suspected Voshparlet precisely."

"Whoa! Hold on!" I shook my head to clear it. "This is all going a little fast for me. What exactly is going on here?"

Grshluk took a seat and motioned for me to sit where the deceased had lately sat.

"No time for pleasantries. Sit and let's make plans while we still have time."

"You mean…?" Burevost paled.

"I mean only that if a message was sent, we have very little time." He turned to me and introduced to the group and them to me. Burevost was the leader of this cell and the members were Anplismak, Yuriopster, Gulrishmet, and Marlikaspan. And, no, I did not catch all the names the first time through. My head was still spinning from the rapid succession of events so soon after the terrors of the tunnel.

Yes, I guess I was shell-shocked.

While I mused over my state of shock, Grshluk was apprising his confederates on the current status of our invasion.

"Oh dear!" Marlikaspan wrung his hands. "The human forces are growing! How soon until they reach the critical mass?"

Grshluk waved off the question. "What we need to concern ourselves with is what can we do now to aid the humans in defeating Klakmonidos?"

"Who knows?" Anplismak shrugged. "We know nothing of their potentialities. How can we possibly design support for such an unknown?"

Burevost tried to forestall any hysterics. "I think Grshluk is looking for general ideas rather than campaign specifics. What resources have we to offer?"

"Let me say first," Grshluk motioned toward me, "this human's companion has gone to inform their leaders about the trap prepared by Klakmonidos. We need to find some way to assist them and extricate them from the doom that awaits. Some distraction, perhaps?"

Gulrishmet raised a hand. "Our resources in the city are limited so any distraction would be minimal. And I fear any such attempt would be met harshly by Klakmonidos' adherents. We must be circumspect."

Yuriopster scowled. "But do we have the luxury of time to be so circumspect?"

"I am afraid," the leader said, "as limited as the resources are, we have to coordinate some sort of action or all our hopes will be lost."

"Certainly." Anplismak nodded. "We can inform…"

Hearing something in the distance, I had turned my head away from the conversation. Grshluk leaned toward me.

"What is the matter, human?"

I looked around at the faces. "Doesn't anyone hear that? What is that strange noise?"

Yuriopster leaped to his feet, overturning his chair in the process. "It is the Security Police! We must hide!"

Everyone was up in a flash and Grshluk had the door opened. "We must leave quickly and spread out. Human, follow me into the woods."

Everyone else cleared the building in a heartbeat, spreading out in all directions with Grshluk crouch-running through the crops, heading for the woods.

Without looking around to see if the security forces were close enough to detect our departure, I kept my head down and raced after the sounds of Grshluk through the field. At some point, I got the goggles back on my face so I could see better where I was going. Still, the sound of the demons footfalls leading the way were getting further and further away.

A voice drifted back over the field. "Hurry! We must not be captured."

Straining to keep up, I couldn't say anything but I was thinking that I was running as fast as my short legs can go.

Further away I heard, "Faster! They are getting closer!"

A few moments later, I burst through the last of the crops and entered the woods in a dead run. Once I was sure the foliage overhead would successfully hide my position, I slowed down and looked around.

I saw no sign of Grshluk.

Stopping, I listened intently.

No footfalls. No sounds of a demon stumbling through any underbrush.

Only the sounds of my own breathing.

Well, that and the noise back at the barn where the security forces had arrived.

CHAPTER TWELVE

Lost and alone in the woods.

A situation familiar in nightmares or children's fairy tales but not something one imagines they will encounter in the real world. Or even in an unreal world like this place.

I stood silently for a time but could hear nothing moving. Had Grshluk simply found a spot to hide? A place he knew where he could not be discovered? If so, I wish he had told me about it before the coffee clatch in the barn. Amazing how poorly executed this affair was. "No planning" usually had very poor results and this adventure was a case in point.

A few minutes of listening led me to try and looking for footprints or some other sign of where my guide had gotten himself to.

No such luck.

I knew that somewhere, in some direction from my position, the Allied troops were closing in on a major disaster while I was here playing hide-and-seek in the woods.

The situation made me really aware how neat a thing telepathy could have been right about then. Sure, the spy's telepathy had brought the problem on us, but the ability could certainly help me find my way out of the woods.

I thought of going back to the barn and retracing our steps or maybe those of another member of the group but, from the sounds I was hearing, more security forces had arrived and were beating the brush to find us.

Amazing to think that Klakky had enough resources to spend on such a minor thing even as the soldiers were being lured into the trap.

Using the noise from the security forces, I moved away from them deeper and deeper into the woods. From some vague recall, I thought I was moving back toward the metropolis. If nothing else, perhaps I could make it back to my unit and find out if Bennett had been successful in his mission to forestall the second wave.

After a time of movement, I got the impression that I should have been out of the woods by now. I stopped and looked around and realized I was completely, if not totally, lost. So, I sat down on a log and tried to think things through.

I knew that without close contact with the underground there was no way I could coordinate with Bennett. Our troops would stumble after the bait set by the demons, enter the causeway and get pummeled by whatever evil weapon Satan had created.

Although I hated to think about it, things didn't look too good for the visiting team.

While thus occupied in some well-deserved self-pity, a movement between some trees in the distance caught my eye. Raising my weapon, I dropped behind the log and looked intently where I had detected motion. Presently, a woman came into view. Yes, a human female. From what I could recall, there were no female troops included in this mission, unless I had overlooked something. She was looking from side to side like she had lost something.

If nothing else, she looked as lost as me. Standing, I waved my arms over my head to get her attention without having to yell. There was no telling how close any security troops might be.

After a few moments, she noticed my frantic waving and made a bee-line to my position. I met her halfway.

"What unit are you with?" I asked when she was within speaking distance.

"Unit? What are you talking about?" She laughed.

Now that she was closer, I wondered at her clothes. Like nothing I had seen before except in old movies and such. For all I knew, that retro look was coming back.

"You're not with the invasion force, are you? Then how did you get here? Who are you?"

She stopped a couple of paces in front of me. "I am Veronica Symington and I got here by escaping from Purgatory." She glanced around. "I seem to have gotten separated from my friend."

"Purgatory? What's that? Isn't it just another name for Hell?"

She laughed as though I had done something humorous. "Not really. Purgatory is the place in Hell where the souls are tormented for eternity."

"Yeah, and you escaped from there?"

"Yes, me and Elizabeth. This is my second time but the first for Elizabeth." She looked around again. "I certainly hope the poor thing hasn't gotten lost."

"The second time? So how did you get back into Purgatory?"

She shrugged. "They captured me again. Just like the first time, I just can't figure out where to go, how to get out of here. I always wind up in the woods with no markers to lead to the exit." Another glance around. "I was hoping that the two of us might be able to figure it out but now I seem to have misplaced her."

"So, how did you get here to begin with?"

Her eyes locked on mine while a smirk played with the corner of her mouth. "First of all, I died."

I stumbled backward a step. "Wait! You're a ghost?"

"Yes, I suppose I am."

"That's crazy! I've never seen a ghost." Shifting my head to one side and the other, I stared at her. "Shouldn't I be able to see through you or something?"

"I don't know. Perhaps we can manifest easier in this realm. Anyway, I remember waiting for the angels to arrive and take me to Heaven, or to rise to the Pearly Gates. Whatever. When that didn't happen, I found myself here and I was quickly captured and put into Purgatory. I assumed I had been sent here by God."

"And what horrible sins did you think got you sent here?"

Another shrug. "I've never been sure of that. Perhaps I was prideful. Perhaps I was not as charitable as I should have been. I really cannot say for certain. It's not like they tell you why you're here."

Shaking my head, I said, "That's doesn't sound anything like I what I was told to expect. Surely they would have a judgment or something and tell you why you were being condemned." I followed her gaze left and right, looking for her friend. "Uh, you didn't happen to see a demon pass through here anytime recently, did you?"

"Why? Was he chasing you?"

Glancing around, I said, "No, I'm working with him to…"

She quickly stepped back, raising a hand to ward me off. "You're… you're working with them!?" Her eyes were wide.

"Oh, hell, no!" I laughed. "No, you don't understand. I'm with the U. S. Army and we invaded Hell this afternoon to end the reign of Klak-… well, Satan. Grshluk and a few friends are on our side trying to stop Satan. The bad demons attacked us and we fled into this forest. And now I seem to have lost him." I glanced around again. "I was hoping maybe you had seen him come through here. We have to coordinate our efforts with the local underground to defeat… Satan."

Her hand had lowered but the eyes were still wide. "You mean you came into Hell to save us?"

"Lady," I laughed again, "as far as I know we were only here to defeat Satan. We weren't told anything about rescuing any souls. Come to think of it, nobody mentioned anything about there even being souls here to rescue."

She stared. "What did you think Hell was for? How could you not know about the tortured souls being kept here?"

"Lady… Veronica," my turn to raise my hands, "our mission was to stop Satan. I'm sure if the mission planners had thought about it further they might have seen the need to save the souls as well. Maybe they figured it would just naturally occur once Satan was defeated. I don't know."

"But now that you're here…?"

"I've really got enough on my plate at the moment. The Army is walking into a trap and I've gotta find Grshluk so the demons can help us before Satan brings about the end of the world."

She bit her lip. "Maybe you should ask Augie."

"And who is this Augie character?"

"Augie. He's the guy I told you about – I think I mentioned him – he's escaped from Purgatory more than anyone I know. He's the one who helped me the last time I escaped. If it hadn't been for him, I wouldn't have thought it possible."

"That's great, but I don't need to know how to escape from Purgatory." I shook my head. "All I need to know at present is how to get back in touch with the underground before the world is destroyed."

"It's not just that. He knows a lot about this place. Like I said, he's escaped more than anyone. I'm sure he could help."

Time was running short and I had to do something. "But how's that going to help the cause?"

"Maybe just trying to round up all the escaped souls will keep Satan and his demons busy for a while."

Not bad, I thought. "Hmm, that might be good for the diversion we need if nothing else. So, how do we find this Augie character?"

Her attention was distracted again and she surveyed the woods, stretching her neck for a better view. "Actually, I had hoped to find him out here – this is where I've found him before – but I think he's gotten captured again. Hopefully, Elizabeth hasn't been recaptured already. It seems it always takes them awhile to notice anyone's escaped."

"Captured? You mean, like, back in Purgatory?"

"Yes, of course." She glared as if I was addle-brained or something. "What aren't you understanding? We try to escape from Purgatory and the demons come and put us back. It's not too hard to grasp, is it?"

"No, not at all but I was hoping he was in the woods somewhere. I don't think I have time to plan breaking into Purgatory as well as…"

Her laughter cut me off. High and lilting. It was so sharp in the general silence that I was certain the security forces might have heard it. "Silly! Getting into Purgatory is simple. They don't expect anyone to try and break into the place."

"Yeah, but once inside, we'll have to fight our way back out."

Her smirk was evident. "Do I look like I could fight my way out… alone? It's not going to be that difficult. Believe me."

While I was considering this, another noise came from my left. I turned, fully expecting to see Grshluk making a timely reappearance. No, it was another female.

"Elizabeth!" Veronica rushed forward and embraced her friend. "I was so afraid they had recaptured you already."

"No, but I lost track of you rather quickly. If it hadn't been for your laughter… What is this place?" Her eyes stopped on me. "And who is that? One of Augie's friends?"

"No, he… Sorry, I didn't catch your name."

"It's Eric. Eric Patterson."

"Thank you. And this is my friend, Elizabeth Larkspur." She turned back to her friend. "These are the woods where I always encountered Augie before. But he's not here. I think he may have been captured again."

"Oh, dear. What are we going to do then?"

Veronica beamed toward me. "This young man is going to help us get Augie out. It would appear the American army has invaded to defeat Satan and free us all."

Elizabeth stared at me. "The army can do this?" She blinked a couple of times. "Then why haven't they done it before now?"

Good question, I thought.

CHAPTER THIRTEEN

While I was strolling through the woods with two attractive dead ladies, Bennett was having his own form of fun as well. I am sure he would have preferred the company I was keeping, even if they were dead. At least neither of my companions would have bitten his head off.

Since Bennett's report dove-tailed with what he was seeing on the ground, Captain Anderson had ordered all units to stand firm pending further orders.

The Captain re-seated the radio and sighed again.

"Everything okay, sir?" Bennett was looking a bit worried. "No conflicting orders yet, are there?"

"No, son, but there's not a unit out there they can move from their position even if they wanted to. Either the General will accept your intel and revise the plan or," he shrugged, "or we'll free everyone up with the final wave coming into the mix."

Bennett nodded and followed the Captain topside again.

The Major lowered his clipboard when they arrived and looked from one to the other while he chewed his lip a moment as if deciding whether to risk his career on taking the news to the General. After a minute's consideration, he nodded. "Let's take a walk."

Major Hopkins had them accompany him to mention the intel to Ironguts. Bennett tagged along in their wake which was a far gutsier decision that I would have cared to act upon. I would have begged off and returned to the action below. Still, it was interesting that he got to witness the interchange.

Ironguts was hunkered over a map discussing their advance with his adjutant. He glanced up as they arrived.

Saluting smartly, Major Hopkins said, "General, I believe you might be interested in some intel here we've received from Captain Anderson."

Ironguts nodded disinterestedly to Anderson. "Captain?"

The Captain saluted before saying, "Yes, sir. One of our units has interrogated one of the demons and discovered a trap being laid by the enemy, sir. They have a plan of operation to draw our troops into an ambush, when the troops reach a position on the wide avenue in front of the Citadel. All the units with which we have presently engaged are being held in position. None of the enemy is pressing the issue at any point of our insertion. It would appear they are waiting for something."

Ironguts sneered. "It should appear obvious, *gentlemen*, that the enemy is in a holding pattern waiting for their own reinforcements. Isn't that normally why such tactics are utilized?"

"Well, uh, yes, sir, normally," Hopkins was evidently rattled, "but taken with the intel from the prisoner…"

"Mister," with his jaw clenched, Ironguts seemed to be spitting out the words, "one such prisoner is called black intel… disinformation. Have you got a second prisoner that corroborates this claim?" His stern look seared first one officer and then the other. Bennett was, fortunately, standing out of the action and remained unscathed, beyond the kill range of the glare.

"No, sir." Both officers replied together.

"Very good then, Major." He glared at Anderson. "*Captain*, you'd best get back to your post and coordinate the invasion… unless some local 'friendly' lobster has told you to expect a shipment of flowers and bon-bons within the hour."

"Yes, sir!" Anderson saluted sharply and turned to leave, his face red.

Bennett turned to follow but heard:

"And Major Hopkins, could I see you in the command tent for a moment?"

Gratefully, the two climbed through the portal and descended to the street once more.

"Sorry, Wainwright, but you can see I have no influence over the marching orders." He shook his head. "The General seems dead-set to bring the final wave regardless of the apparent dangers."

"I understand, sir, but there might be something else I can help with. I am sure my partner is in contact with the friendly underground despite what the General thinks and I am certain there will be some of their number coming to assist us. Can I at least remain here to help identify them when they arrive?"

He grunted. "You mean, if they are going to arrive?" He shook his head. "It's not exactly going against orders to allow you to stay, Wainwright, because I think there is something fishy about this entire thing." He looked around, sniffing, and nodded. "Yes, there is definitely some stench here. Wainwright, you can stay in case those non-existent friendlies do show up." He winked.

"Thank you, sir." He turned to leave and stopped. "One other thing, sir, I notice you seem to be having trouble coordinating all the units."

He pointed to his helmet. "It's the jammers, son. We don't want the enemy interfering so they only call in occasionally."

Bennett nodded. "Well, sir, one thing about those jammers…"

CHAPTER FOURTEEN

We trekked through the forest. The women were talking in low voices most of the time. What snatches of the conversation I caught sounded like they were discussing fashion. Whatever for, given their condition, I couldn't understand.

"Excuse me, Veronica," I spoke during one of the lulls, "I was wondering when it was… well, when did you…"

She laughed. "It's all right to ask. It was 1954 when I passed over. Doesn't seem that long, now, but I don't even know what year it is back there."

"It was 2028 when the mission started. I was born back in 2005, if that helps anything."

"Wow! That would mean I'm old enough to be your grandmother."

"Yeah, or my great-grandmother."

She stopped and placed her hands on her hips. "Watch it, young man. It is not polite to discuss a woman's age."

"I only meant…" I swallowed hard. "Sorry, ma'am."

They both stared at me while I felt the crimson glow spread. Then they both laughed.

Elizabeth said, "He's cute when he blushes like that."

"Yes." She turned to me. "I was born in 1926 and was twenty-eight when I passed. There was some difficulty with delivering my second child." She sighed and shrugged. "I have always wondered whatever became of my family."

"Well, perhaps when you get to the better place you can find out more." I grinned. "I don't think this place allows much in the way in communication with the outside world."

"Yes, perhaps when I get to heaven." She nodded toward the other ghost. "Elizabeth could have been my great-grandmother. She was born when Thomas Jefferson was President."

My eyes bulged. "Wow, that's amazing! So the two of you had a first-hand view at so much of our history. I wish we had more time to talk but I think we had better get along with our mission before it's too late."

"Right you are, young man," Elizabeth motioned forward, "lead on."

After we got moving again, I asked Veronica, "We're going back to Purgatory to find this Augie fellow. Is it a big place? How will you know where to find him?"

"Big?" She exchanged glances with her friend. "I would say the structure does not look too very big…"

"From the outside." Elizabeth laughed.

"But from the inside," Veronica nodded firmly, "it looks so very much larger."

Elizabeth shuddered. "Amazing how much evil they can cram into such a small space."

Veronica hugged her shoulders. "I know, dear, but hopefully it will all soon be a thing of the past."

We walked a bit further before I asked, "So, with the size of the building being so large, how will we know where to find this guy?"

Veronica's answer was immediate. "They'll have him in the lowest level."

"How do you know that?"

"Those who attempt escape are always put back in a lower chamber after re-indoctrination. And since Augie was re-captured in the Citadel…"

"In the Citadel itself!! Where Satan lives? What was he doing there?"

She thought a moment, "When I first met him in the forest, he said he thought he knew how to combat Satan and get everyone out of Purgatory." She shrugged. "He did not go into any detail but if that was what he was up to, that was enough, I figure, to get him put in the lowest level."

It was my turn to shudder. "Whoa! That must be real bad down there!"

Elizabeth and Veronica both nodded. "We can only imagine."

I thought about it for a while as we walked. I had no idea how to get back in touch with Grshluk or the underground. I was too far away from Bennett to get word to him without having to battle all the demon forces between me and him. Here was a guy who had already been into the Citadel. Even if his plan was a patchwork cuckoo, the data he might be able to give me about the Citadel could be a life-saver.

If only I could get to him soon enough.

For all I knew at that time, Bennett had been arrested for desertion and clapped into the brig. Who knew what was happening over there?

This Augie fellow may be a long shot but at the moment it seemed to be the only shot I had. And at least I did not have to worry about the physical safety of my comrades. They were already dead.

Now I just had to keep myself from joining that fraternity.

"And you think this Augie actually has a plan?"

"That's what he said." Veronica said it with such conviction that I couldn't help but grin ear to ear.

"Okay, you've sold me. Let's go get him."

It did not appear to matter how far we had already walked or how much further we had to go but I think all of our steps got a bit lighter, bouncier from that point forward.

That is, if ghosts were actually capable of walking on the ground.

CHAPTER FIFTEEN

As our steps got bouncier, Bennett was still creating a ruckus over at the command post. I'm glad he had that job as I probably wouldn't have had the gumption he did to *push* his ideas with the brass.

Bennett was kneeling beside the Captain's aide, Serjeant Wong, in the street about two blocks from the command post. Captain Anderson was squatting behind them and leaned forward to whisper. "If you're wrong about this, Bennett, at least I won't have to worry about facing the General's wrath."

Bennett grimaced and whispered over his shoulder, "No, sir, none of us will."

Wong looked nervously back at the Captain.

The Captain nodded. "So, Bennett, our headsets are off and none of the bastards have come up to attack us yet. We've sat here thinking as loud as possible and they don't seem to notice anything. So far, so good. What sort of proof do you suggest?"

Peeking around the corner, Bennett scoped out the street and pulled back to report. "Sir, there is one of the larger fellows just ahead, standing behind a small section of wall. He seems to shoot occasionally but otherwise is just standing there and waiting. Perhaps if the Serjeant could take off his boots and sneak up on the fellow…?"

He could hear the Serjeant gulp.

"Well, Wong, what do you think?"

After a moment, the Serjeant started taking off his boots. The Captain nodded at Bennett. "Get ready to give him cover."

Gripping his rifle, Bennett gave him the thumbs up.

The Captain nodded in return. "You ready, Serjeant?" Wong nodded. "Then let's get this over with."

Setting the boots to one side, Wong stood and gave Bennett a glance that said "you sure about this?" Bennett nodded in reply to the unasked question.

Wong eased around the corner moving quietly, slowly on tiptoes.

Bennett got in a prone position, keeping his weapon on the demon, while the Captain edged into a position to watch the experiment better.

The Serjeant tiptoed slowly closer to the demon. When the demon began to turn, Wong froze where he was, sweat dripping from his chin onto the cobblestone pavement. The vignette held for only a moment, long though it seemed, before the demon faced forward again.

Wong let out his breath slowly and waited a few seconds before advancing again. When it looked to Bennett like the Serjeant was going to tap the fellow on the shoulder, Wong turned around, looking tense, and tiptoed quickly back to the corner where the other waited.

Shaking, he leaned heavily against the building.

Bennett pulled back from the cover position and patted the fellow on the shoulder. Then, "Well, Captain, what now? Care to try it again with the helmet head-set on?"

Wong reached for his boots as the Captain shook his head.

The three returned quietly to the tent HQ.

He stood to one side as the Captain was talking on the field-set.

"Yes, Lieutenant, I realize this runs counter to your earlier orders. That's why I'm telling you now." He listened for a moment. "No, son, it is not a suggestion, it's an order."

He hung up the phone, sweating visibly. "Serjeant Wong, let me know when the next group calls in."

"Yes, sir."

The Captain turned to Bennett and shook his head. "I sure hope your intel about the headsets is correct, Wainwright. Otherwise the General will have my scalp." He grunted. "And more than likely have it mounted next to your balls on his office wall."

Bennett winced. "Well, sir, it worked for both Eric and I. And you witnessed Sergeant Wong here. He walked right up behind the demon and the guy never knew he was there." He nodded. "Like I discovered, they actually hear the static and can target our men because of it."

Captain Anderson shook his head. "I've been in a lot of action in my time, son, but I find myself shaken by the strange turns this campaign had taken. And that my career could very well be hanging on the correctness of my decisions – and that in the eyes of the General – is enough to turn my skin gray." He sighed. "I suppose all we can do now is wait until the demons start falling back. All the units have been told to proceed cautiously at that point. Is there anything else we need to do?"

Bennett shrugged. "Not that I can think of, sir. I'm just waiting for Eric to get word to me about what's going on." He glanced along the streets running away from the command post. "I don't know what's keeping the underground from contacting us. The guys are telepaths we were told and should be able to get to someone immediately. I should have thought someone would have contacted us by now. I just hope nothing's gone wrong for Eric."

The Captain glanced at his watch. "Well, soldier, we can hold out until the General gives the order to move. After that…" He shrugged.

Bennett gulped. "Understood, sir. I just hope they get here before it's too late or none of this will mean anything."

The Captain grunted. "Buck up, soldier. The battle ain't over til the fat demon sings."

Bennett cringed while the Captain and Serjeant laughed.

CHAPTER SIXTEEN

While Bennett kept abreast of the goings on at HQ, unknown to me at the time, I was walking through the forest chit-chatting with the girls about food, of all things. Elizabeth, especially, was regaling us about dishes she loved that had not passed into future generations.

Likewise, she was amazed with the widespread delicacy of our time: ice cream.

"I had tried one of the ices once when I went to the Capital City," she said, "it was for the inauguration of Andrew Jackson, I believe."

"You knew Andrew Jackson!"

She drew back. "Know him? Young man, I was a merchant's daughter not connected with the government or the army. I did not know the man though I did have the opportunity to hear him speak."

"What did he sound like?"

She thought a moment. "It had a mountainy twang to it, I recall. Strange accent but the timbre of the voice was a rumbling baritone. Forceful. It carried out over the crowd easily."

"Man, I would have loved to have heard it. He was one of my heroes when I was a kid." Something ahead tugged at my attention. "What's that? Do you hear that?"

"That's probably just the river." Veronica nodded. "It means we're getting close."

Eric stopped and cocked an ear to front. "A river? That sounds like a mighty big one. How are we going to get across?"

"Normally," Elizabeth said, "we just float across… but I suppose that won't work for you."

"Not unless you can carry me!"

Veronica pointed to the left. "I believe there is a bridge across closer toward Purgatory." Nodding toward Elizabeth, "You probably didn't see it, this being your first time out."

"Okay, ma'am, if you could lead the way."

They followed Veronica through the thinning trees.

"You seem to have a well-developed sense of direction," I spoke while following. "I know it may have something to do with you being a spirit and all but a lot of people I know could get lost in a shopping mall much less this forest."

Veronica fell back beside him. "It's a knack, I suppose, but different places have different feelings to me and I can 'feel' Purgatory over there," she pointed, "and so the bridge must be just beyond it."

"I wonder," I muttered to myself, "if the military knows about this 'sense of space' thing."

And, as expected, the trees thinned a bit more and there was Purgatory, looming on the opposite bank of the very wide river, still some distance from our position. The structure was white, apparently about four stories tall without any windows. The structure seemed ovoid… curved, rather than having any squared corners.

The bridge was just before us. It was about twenty feet wide and had a railing along each side only about a foot high. Far too easy to fall over and, even worse, no good at offering cover.

And we were just about completely out of trees.

My weapon at the ready, I glanced around. "I don't like being exposed like this."

"I doubt they'll have anyone watching this area." Veronica motioned us forward. "It's not like people are beating a path to Purgatory. It's a place they'd rather stay clear of. Even most the demons."

I'm sure I scowled as I said, "Yeah, I heard the same thing about Hell. Yet here I am, and voluntarily."

Both the women laughed at that.

As we started across the bridge, my senses were on high alert, eyes scanning the building and the surrounding countryside. Glancing left, I could see the city. It seemed too damned close for my likes. Turning to Veronica, the smile in her eyes defused my rather obvious worry. It died on my lips and I shrugged.

Something about Purgatory bothered me. "So, where's the entrance to the building? I don't see a door anywhere."

She pointed to the left. "It's on the other side."

Stopping near the halfway point, no longer concerned with being seen, I stared from the building back to Veronica. "Which other side? The back side?"

"No. The left side." She pointed again.

"Wait! You mean the side facing the city? The citadel?" She nodded, smirking. "You mean where Satan can see?"

"I seriously doubt he's going to be looking this way. Like I said…"

"Yeah, I know. Nobody's gonna try and break into the place." Scowling, I fidgeted with the rifle and looked back at Purgatory. "I just hope you're right." With a sigh, I shrugged and resumed progress across the river.

On the opposite bank was another stand of trees beyond the wide path leading to the object of our expedition.

"Even though you're certain no one will be looking this direction, I'd still feel safer if we had some cover." I pointed across the river. "We'll get into those trees and approach the building from the opposite flank. That way, even if someone comes out for a cigarette break or something, we won't be spotted."

"Cigarette break?" Elizabeth laughed.

"Yes," I said, "don't you know what those are?"

"Of course, they were around in my day. But I doubt any of the demons ever get a 'break'."

"Oh, I see." I shrugged. "Let's get this done before we run out of time."

I led the way, double-timing it across the broad expanse of the bridge and into the cover of the trees on the far bank. Turning, I had to wait for my companions who were taking a more leisurely pace.

When they arrived, I asked, "Do y'all always float along at a constant speed?"

They exchanged glances. "We hadn't thought about that." Veronica shrugged. "We were just following."

"Oh, okay." I turned to the left. "Let's do this thing."

Looking puzzled, Elizabeth asked Veronica, "What other thing would we be doing?"

Veronica shook her head. "Pay no mind. Just another of his endearing expressions, I believe. Come on."

It was not very far before the trees began to thin again. "Veronica, do you know how close the trees get to the building?"

"I'm not certain about the back side…" She chuckled and shook her head. "I'm not real good with distances but I think the forest ends a couple of hundred yards from Purgatory."

"And you're certain there won't be any lookouts?"

"I've never seen any. Once I got free of the chamber I was held in, I never encountered anyone, demon or human." She shook her head. "And it is quite a walk from the chamber to the exit." Elizabeth was nodding her agreement.

Eyes widening, I am sure, I shook my head again. "That's so weird! So how did they know you had escaped? Do they have a cell check or anything?"

"No, I have heard that recapture usually only occurs when the escapee accidentally comes across one of Satan's minions."

"That's crazy!"

The two women exchanged glances but didn't respond.

Here the trees did not thin much. It appeared as though the area had been cleared for the construction of the building and the boundary was sliced out of the forest. I was able to stand just behind a tree and examine the building.

"You're right. It looks like a couple of hundred yards to Purgatory. If it's that large building there."

She chuckled. "Yes. That's Purgatory. There's no other building around."

"Just thought I'd check," I said, nodding. "I wasn't sure if there was a group of buildings over here or just the one. From the other angle, I wasn't sure." Yeah, it sounded a bit lame but what else could I say?

She smirked. "Yes, there's just the one."

I nodded and looked around at the lay of the land. It was an open field with absolutely nothing for protection. If this wasn't Hell and I did not have the two women's assurances, I would have thought racing across the distance would be suicide.

But I had to keep the reconnaissance short. Somewhere Bennett and Grshluk – or so I hoped in the latter's case – were working to prevent disaster and I had to do something to help.

I grit my teeth and ran toward the building half-crouched, wondering if I should advance in a serpentine pattern or not. I settled for a flat-out sprint. Reaching the wall, I plastered my back against it making myself as thin as possible. Across the field, I could see the two women sauntering to join me. They both seemed to be smirking now. I tried to ignore the fact and motioned them to hurry up. Time was getting short and I still had no idea how much longer this escapade was going to take.

As they got closer, I said, "I think we ought to pick up the pace a little bit. The army may be walking into the trap already and I haven't even reached this Augie fellow." I grimaced. "And I am not even sure he is going to be able to help anyway."

Veronica walked past, continuing around the building's back side and said, "Yes, I am sure he can help. And it really isn't going to take that long to find him, of that I am certain."

Following the pair – running ahead would only increase my anxiety – we went around the building until we came upon the steps leading up to the small entryway. No guard towers, no sentinels, no one.

Elizabeth dropped back beside me. "From the river side they have a ramp. For bringing in heavy equipment, I suppose."

"Yeah," my tone must surely have said 'just passing the time or else I will scream', "who likes to carry heavy equipment upstairs?"

"Relax, soldier, we're almost there." From her tone I could tell it was accompanied by yet another smirk.

Seems to me women must have smirked more in days gone by. At least modern women still smirk at the same thing: men. I glanced over at Veronica as we ascended; she was shaking her head. I suppose that sort of thing accompanies a smirk.

When we finally reached the entry, I pressed myself to one side in order to glance around and assure myself the way was clear. I don't know why I bothered following normal combat protocols, the women were standing in plain view before the entry, waiting patiently for me to quit "fooling around" and open the door.

To cover any embarrassment, I asked, "What will we encounter?"

Veronica looked at Elizabeth. "I think she should be the one to tell you about the upper levels. After several escapes I have been moved down a few levels where things change slowly. I think the upper levels are used for experimentation. You know, testing techniques and such."

I must've rolled my eyes. The thought of the operators of hell refining their techniques was just a little weird.

Elizabeth was talking. "It is odd, when I first came here, most of the areas I inhabited were very hot… deserts, forest fires, boiling lava, and such. Now they seem to favor colder habitats. Blizzards, frozen tundra, and the like."

My laughter stopped her.

"Young man, it is no laughing matter."

"Oh, I know, ma'am, I know." I fought to regain my composure. "It's just like the old saying. 'When Hell freezes over.' I just thought it was funny."

"Hmph! Well, you just try moving around with your feet encased in frozen blocks of water! Then you can tell me how humorous it seems."

"Yes, ma'am. Sorry for my levity." I moved to the door. "Shall we?" I glanced back to see if they were ready.

After glaring at me again, Elizabeth nodded toward the door. I opened it, trying not to look too wary, and she took the lead. Veronica followed.

Then I entered Purgatory.

Damn! I don't even like the sound of that.

CHAPTER SEVENTEEN

The entryway was nothing more than a corridor curving to the right, slowly descending. No guards, no functionaries with clipboards, and not even the obligatory booth under a sign saying "Information" and displaying a colorful map with a large spot and the legend declaring "you are here".

"See? No guards." Veronika spread her arms. "But I see you're still nervous."

"Yeah, I know. And I don't think I'm going to be any less nervous by being in the building. But at least Satan won't be able to see me in here."

Elizabeth snorted. "Told you. I've never seen anyone at the entrance."

"Okay. You're right again. But you don't have to worry because you're already dead. They can still kill me, you know."

The women exchanged glances. Veronica said, "Yes, that's true but neither of us want to be recaptured. You have no idea how painful that can be." Elizabeth just nodded.

Re-gripping my rifle, I nodded. The way forward was so obvious that even I could not stall by asking which direction. I motioned to Elizabeth. She nodded and led on. Veronica fell in beside me.

"What's really funny," she spoke quietly, "is that there are so many souls in Purgatory that they lose track of a lot of them. One time I escaped into the woods I was gone for… my, it seemed like a couple of weeks, at least. If I had not run into one of Satan's minions I might still be wandering around out there."

"There are that many here?"

She nodded. "You have to figure how many millions of people have lived before your time on the planet. They all passed over…" She shrugged. "I figure that a large number of those souls wound up in here."

"Wow!"

She nudged me, grinning. "Have you ever seen a million people in one place at any one time?"

"I remember seeing films of a Chinese arena that seated over a million but other than that," I shrugged, "I can't even conceive of such a thing."

The corridor curved to the left and began descending. Elizabeth was several steps ahead of us and looking straight ahead. There was no sign of any doors or rooms as far as we could see along the corridor ahead.

Leaning toward Veronica, I spoke softly. "I'm sorry I don't understand it but I don't. If you're a spirit, what can they do to you?"

She turned and stared at me as though I was an imbecile who suddenly popped up from nowhere. "Are you kidding? Enough, believe me. Just like the priests tell you, eternal torture. Didn't you ever wonder about that when you heard about it? Didn't you wonder then how souls could be tortured?"

"I suppose not. But I rarely questioned any of those beliefs. They were just beliefs. You either believed or you didn't. There was no idea of trying to figure out how it could happen. That would make as much sense to me as arguing whether the days of creation were really weeks, months, years, or whatever. It was just another article of faith."

"Well, believe you me, it's something you want to avoid."

The corridor continued its slow descent before us. So far we had not encountered even a single door. And, thankfully, no demons, either.

A sudden thought came to me. "Oh, yeah, the seven levels…"

"The what?"

"Don't you remember hearing about the seven levels of Hell. It was from Dante, I think."

"Levels, hmm. If you could call it that."

"Well, maybe not levels exactly as this hall is sloping but it does go down gradually. Does it do this all the way?"

"All the way down."

"And Augie is being held where?"

She nodded once. "All the way down."

Ahead, a doorway appeared in the curve. Elizabeth continued past but I slowed, bringing my rifle up to ready. Veronica continued as well but I stopped at the doorway and peeked around the corner.

Inside, I could see the back of a demon standing at a small pedestal. He was looking out over a vast chamber where souls floating in the dark were lit up by flashes of lightning. Screams and moans accompanied each of the blasts.

Tiptoeing past the doorway, I quickly caught up to Veronica.

"What was that place?"

She glanced over her shoulder. "That would be one of the indoctrination rooms. The souls are shocked until they become disoriented. It makes them more docile for the duration of the captivity."

"Just electric shock!?"

She nodded. "Yes, that and the constant reminder that you are in Hell because you deserve it. After a while, all the souls begin to believe they belong here and submit quietly."

After letting the thought sink in, my jaw dropped. "Jesus!" I didn't notice the irony of the exclamation. "Our religious upbringing makes us suckers for that tactic. We are always being told that we are sinners." I shook my head. "Every Sunday I remembered hearing that being drilled into us. Damn! The preachers are setting everyone up for this indoctrination! Who're they working for anyway?"

"Search me." Veronica shrugged. "It is possible that some demons have influenced the religious spokespeople over the years. Still, if the people have bought into the story… who's to blame?"

I stared at her. "You'd blame the people rather than the priests? In the Middle Ages, the church pretty much ruled most of Europe, and all the schools of thought. There wasn't any other way to think of the universe. They controlled everyone's concept of reality." Disgusted, I shook my head. "And what about that Torquemada fellow? Was he human or was he one of those demons who escaped to our side?"

She seemed unmoved. "It is still a personal choice if you want to believe in that sort of world." She nodded toward the room we had passed. "I was not what you would call a very religious person but, after some time in the indoctrination, I began to think maybe they were right. How else would I arrive in this place unless I had been so sinful?"

"And you believe that?"

Her laughter was almost mocking. "Of course not! I would like to see you take the torture for several years. You might also buy into the notion. After a while, you cannot help but believe maybe it's true."

She turned and followed after Elizabeth.

Turning back to the room, I chewed my lip a moment, tensing my grip on the weapon before hurrying to catch up to the girls.

They had just passed the second portal. I slowed and glanced in. There was a single demon watching pits of fire and what looked like a volcano in the distance.

Elizabeth must have paused to wait for us because she and Veronica were walking side by side. I pulled up beside the pair. "How big is this place? That volcano looked a couple of miles away, at least!"

Elizabeth seemed to have lightened up a bit as this question actually brought out a smile. "I'm not sure. It seems that both time and distance play tricks on you in this place. Like I said, I had no idea I had been in here as long as it appears I have." She looked around the corridor in which we walked. "Seeing the building from the outside, I would not even think it large enough to hold this corridor, much less the size of the rooms we have encountered."

"The rooms further below," Veronica added, "could be explained, perhaps, by a system of underground caverns. But these rooms here…" She shrugged. "It defies logic."

"Yeah," I shook my head, "as if any form of logic applies in this place."

With a motion of her hand, Elizabeth said, "Shall we?"

"Lead on."

It was a bizarre journey and time did seem to stretch out. At times I got worried that we had been trudging our way along the steady slope for a week or more but that was patently ridiculous. The timer in my stomach would have gone clanging had we been away from the chow line for more than twenty-four. I can go quite a while without food but even intense survival training has its limits.

The women, or ghosts, or… well, whatever, glided along the corridor. Their legs moved as if they were walking but I could see their feet never actually touched the floor. The only footsteps I heard were my own.

As we progressed, they seemed to take no notice of the rooms we passed. I suppose they had already visited each in turn and knew the place well enough. I, on the other hand, rubber-necked at every doorway.

At the first few, I plastered myself against the wall near the doorframe and craned a quick peek. All I ever saw was lightning or fire or lava or whatever in the distance. Near the door was always a demon or two and they always had their backs to us. Like the girls said, why would any of them suspect someone was actually trying to scope out the joint?

I later suspected the fellows were always looking busy because they didn't know when the supervisors might come through and check on them. That may not have been a priority in Hell, I know, but it is a very typical reaction on this side of reality.

As time passed, I simply glanced into the rooms as I walked past, spiraling ever downward. Once I was pulled up short and had to stare hard to make out what was happening in this one room. As my cognitive processes kicked in, my stomach sent my throat a nasty-gram. People – or their spirits in human shape – were being disemboweled while others were being speared on spits to be roasted over a slow flame.

As quickly as I tried to get it out of mind, close my eyes and turn away, it was etched in my brain. And, as you'd expect, all thoughts of eating were banished for quite a while.

More doors came with similar horror stories.

After a time, I seemed to get immune to it all.

My female companions had gotten further ahead of me by stages up until then. I quit being the tourist and pushed ahead to rejoin them.

CHAPTER EIGHTEEN

The levels of Purgatory as described in Dante's famous work was not exactly what I walked through but I could understand the allegory. What I couldn't figure out was how the fellow knew so much about the place. Bad dreams? Too much horseradish and onions? A psychic link to the demon world? Who knows?

After a time, I noticed I was beginning to sweat more than I was accustomed.

"It seems to be getting warmer."

Veronica glanced my way and nodded.

Getting no other response, I added, "Am I going to need any special sort of protective gear?"

Elizabeth asked what that meant and Veronica explained quietly. I don't know if loud voices might attract the demons but we didn't test any alarm systems.

Both laughed. Veronica said, "No, I don't think it will get anywhere near that hot here in the corridor. Besides, we told you it was going to get cooler the further down we go. Remember?"

My ears burned from a different sort of heat but I grinned and nodded. "Yeah, that's right. It seems such an odd idea that I guess I forgot." Another less-than-stellar moment for yours-truly Patterson.

They continued to stare for a moment but I turned ahead and kept moving. Shortly, we were back to our previously unbroken trek.

After a bit, I nodded, said, "The temperature seems to have leveled off. In fact, I think it's getting cooler." I gave the "thumbs-up" to Veronica who then had to translate for Elizabeth.

As the temperature continued to drop, the doors seemed to be coming more often, closer together. Glancing in several rooms as we hurried past, I saw a much smaller tableau than the rooms above. The blasts and lightning bolts seemed more intense, more blue like something from a Tesla spectacular, against a darker background. And there seemed to be far fewer screamers than in the rooms overhead.

By turns, the corridor was growing colder. Without even thinking about it I had turned up my collar and held my arms closer to my body, gripping the rifle loosely in cold fingers.

Following behind the girls a few steps, I was brought up suddenly by their abrupt stop and almost crashed into them. Or would it have been through them? In any event, the corridor ended a few feet in front of them. A single portal was off to the right. I stepped up beside Veronica and blew a warm breath into my right hand.

"This must be it. Man, it's cold!"

"Shh!"

She pointed over my shoulder. Turning, I could see the cause of her concern. Advancing to the doorway, I craned my head around the corner to see if there was more.

No. The room was quite small and held only two truncated columns or pedestals with electrically sparking harnesses. Each of the contraptions held a single entity. The demon watching the dials on his readout monitor was probably bored and might notice if I had talked much more. At least the other rooms had enough noise and activity to cover our passage; here, not so much.

After surveying the scene, I whispered to Veronica, "Only the one demon?"

She shrugged. "How should I know? Take him out before he can signal to his friends and let's get out of here."

I tried to keep from rolling my eyes but I don't think I managed it. "Yeah, we don't need the alarm sounding."

Trying to remember if hitting the demon on the head would knock them out or only make them mad, I did the sensible thing: I raised the rifle and squeezed the trigger. The fellow fell instantly with a clean head shot. Hopefully, it was fast enough to prevent any alarms being sent.

Shouldering my weapon, I stepped over the jailer/torturer and looked at the control panel. "Now, how do I shut this thing off?"

Veronica entered the chamber and stepped beside me. "Like this." She pushed a lever down and the sparking and noise stopped. One of the souls, stepped down from his harness. The other spirit seemed a little too dazed to move.

"Ah, Miss Symington, we meet again." He bowed his head over her hand a moment, smiled then seemed to notice Elizabeth and I. "And who are your two young friends?"

"These are two friends from the land where I came from. This is Elizabeth," the fellow bowed over the hand she extended, "and this is Eric."

I shook the extended hand and found it to be somewhat solid. I think if I pressed really hard my fingers would have gone through his but there was at least some substance to him. Not entirely ghostly at all.

I don't think I will ever understand the physics of the situation.

"This young man seems different. I take it he is not among the dearly departed?"

Veronica laughed. "No, if you can believe it, he is with a military expeditionary force who has invaded Hell to eliminate Satan."

Turning to me, he blinked a few times as if to grasp exactly what any of that meant. Then he shook his head.

"I would not have thought such things were possible. But I shall not ask how you came to be here, young Eric, but I am happy to make the acquaintance of another who is an enemy of the Evil One."

"Happy to make your acquaintance. Augie, is it?"

Like some courtier, he bowed. "Augustine of Hippo, at your service."

"Augustine of Hippo!" I turned and glanced at the two women. Calling him "Augie", indeed! "Aren't you a saint or something?"

"I have heard others say that, including Miss Symington here, but that would have been long after I left the Earthly realm."

"Well, yes, I understand that part of it but… I mean, you're a saint? Doesn't that mean you were holy and religious and all that?" I shook my head. "So, what are you doing in Hell?"

His sheepish grin made him look younger than his gray hair advised. "Let us just say that I have no certainty on that matter. What I do know is that when I arrived here, I thought I must have been sent here for the sin of pride. I was a very prideful man, so certain of my piety and my methods of attaining a state of Grace." He raised a hand. "Yes, the errors of the heart can happen to even the most righteous, I suppose, and only Lord God can speak what we never can of our secret places."

"So you have no idea how you got here?"

"I only know that after I passed over, I waited patiently for the heavenly host to arrive and transport me to the throne of God." He spread his arms and his eyes rose upward. After a moment as a statue, he dropped the arms and sighed. "Ah, the vanity I once had!"

"Eric," Elizabeth tapped my shoulder, "I know you'd like to catch up on old times with Augie here but don't you have something more pressing?"

I could have slapped myself!

"Yes, so Augie… Augustine… Sain-…"

"Augie will suffice." He grinned.

"All right. Augie, these women tell me you think you know how to get at Satan."

After making the sign of the cross, he nodded. "Yes, after many years of torment, I came to realize something I should have known from the beginning. It was a revelation in Hell!" His hands came together and he looked upward as if in prayer.

"Yes," I said after a moment, "and what was that?"

Eyes refocusing, his look was intense. "In many of the older writings, the religious fathers spoke of Hell as simply a special place within the heart of Man that has withdrawn from the presence of God. Sinning would naturally separate us from that state of Grace, you see?" He nodded.

Again I waited a moment before, "Yes, but how did that…"

He spread his arms upward, continuing, "When I had that realization, I could suddenly see this was not the realm of Hell as I had been told by these demons. This was something completely divorced from any religious faith. And if this was not the Hell of the Church, it had to be nothing more than a very mundane realm taking advantage of the souls on their way to Heaven!" His eyes blazed. "And once I came to that realization, escape was easy." He lowered his arms and shrugged. "Easy."

"Yes, but you kept getting recaptured."

He shot me a wounded look. "Alas, I could not find the pathway out of this realm." He glanced at the two women. "And I would not leave these other tortured souls in the grasp of these demons. I wanted to take them all with me on my voyage to heaven. If God has issue with such a course, He can deal with it I am certain. And it is with absolute certainty that I say these beasts are not a part of His Divine Plan."

There were parts of his logic that escaped me as to places and plans and all. I would also like to have discussed what I saw as his continuing pride for one thing but we really did not have the time for spiritual dissertations.

"That's quite an amazing tale, your saintship, but we really need to get out of here and stop this fellow everyone thinks is Satan." Nodding toward Veronica, "She said you had a plan. What is it?"

Shaking his head he stepped back. "It was not really much of a plan and certainly not worthy of a military man such as yourself…"

Time was wasting. "Still, I'd like to hear it."

"All right, if you insist." He nodded and stepped forward again. "Every time I had escaped, I felt fear and hate toward the demons when they came to take me back. This last time, however, due to a revelation, I found I could circumvent most of them by admiring them, loving them, unconditionally."

"That's the plan?" Looking at the two women, I could see they were impressed. "That's it? Just spread the love, huh? Well, uh, that's not really much of a plan. Not for my guys, anyway. And I certainly don't think it would fly for General Ironguts and I don't want to be the one to run it past him."

"What do you mean?"

I grunted. "Let's just say my general would not embrace that plan."

He sighed. "I suspected as much. But perhaps it can assist your military adventure by having the souls disrupt the demons in this way. I am certain no one has ever admired Satan, truly loved him, during all the long years of his reign."

"Yeah, I'd say you're correcto-mundo on that little item. The demon I spoke to said he rules by fear alone. Even with his most trusted followers are deathly afraid of him."

Augie had stepped back again, eyes widening. "Wait! What's this? You are friends with a demon?"

"Yeah, the fellow that helped me escape from the city. It seems that a lot of the demons are just regular folk… er, regular demons – I guess – who have been terrorized by this tyrant for centuries. Those who are not his followers are getting fewer in number all the time. They want to be rid of him in the worst way. As much as we would. If not more."

Again, Augie's arms were raised. "It is a sign! The Lord God has shown me the rightness of my convictions." Lowering his arms, he stepped forward to grab my shoulders and look into my eyes. "Do you know what Satan's massive weapon is?"

"Not exactly. But I figure it's a really big gun or power beam of some sort."

He shook his head and laughed. "No! His weapon is the souls in Purgatory. He has found a way to utilize the tormented to power a weapon of destruction." Releasing me, he turned in a circle, staring at the walls. "All of this is nothing more than the power behind his weapon." He grabbed me again. "The more souls we can release, the less powerful his weapon will be. And we may perhaps find a way to use that power for our own means." Releasing me, he motioned toward the exit. "Come. Let's delay no further."

Where Bennett and the troops were at that moment – if he had indeed gotten through with his message – I had no clue. I would like to have said we did not have the time to release all the souls but, if Augie was right, it might be the very thing to save us all.

If he was right.

Augustine left the chamber, Elizabeth and Veronica on his heels. My pause was momentary but I shouldered my rifle and followed after them.

"Wait!" I called out. "So, what's the plan?"

CHAPTER NINETEEN

If I had it bad thinking time was passing too quickly while so little was being done, it must have really been hell for Bennett. He had military procedure and red tape to deal with.

He told me later that the time sitting there waiting for something to happen seemed like a week or two. I don't know if time travels at different rates there in Hell – although if someone proved this point, it should not surprise me in the least – but everything just seemed to take forever.

Bennett had been pacing the command area waiting for the contacts from Grshluk's group to arrive. His obvious agitation was beginning to make several at the HQ a little bit nervous as well.

Serjeant Wong tapped him on the shoulder. "Would you mind sitting down, Wainwright, you're like a first time father in the maternity ward and you're getting everyone a little buggy."

"Oh, sorry, sir. It's just that we still haven't heard from Patterson and we could get the orders to advance at any time."

"I know." Wong turned to see the Captain hang up the headset. "But try and sit down for a while. No one wants to go into action hyped up, y'know."

The Captain came over. "The last of the units have been informed of the situation. They'll be ready to follow the demons when they fall back but they will advance slowly."

"I just hope they do not fall into the trap." Bennett's worries remained evident.

"Don't worry, son." Anderson laughed. "It is an old tactic and one that worked well for William the Conqueror at Hastings, but it won't work here. The men are expecting it."

"That's good, sir."

The Captain set his hands on his hips and leaned backward. Several popping sounds could be heard. "Now, when can we hear some word from your partner?"

"I don't know, sir. I really expected…"

A sudden movement at the side of the Command Post drew their attention. Two demons came from the hull of the building adjacent to the HQ tent, stumbling and sliding down the pile of collapsed rubble. Serjeant Wong raised his weapon.

Seeing the small demons, hands extended in front, twisting at the wrists, Bennett pushed Wong's weapon down.

"Wait! Don't shoot. These are the fellows we've been expecting."

"You're certain?" Captain Anderson had his own sidearm at the ready.

"Yes, I'm positive." Bennett stepped toward the demons who bowed low before him.

Righting themselves, one spoke, "Thank you for not killing us. Who is the one called 'Bennett'?"

"That would be me." Bennett bowed in return and smiled, obviously relieved.

"Greetings from your friend, Grshluk. I am Meshta and this is my friend, Gunrtok. We have heard from Grshluk and he is waiting for your friend Eric to exit from Purgatory and…"

Bennett interrupted. "What!?!"

The other demon, Gunrtok, shrugged. "We thought it most strange to go into such a place but we assumed it was a part of your plan."

"Not any plan that I knew of." Bennett turned to the Captain. "I thought he was with Grshluk, meeting with the resistance."

"I suppose you have not heard… but how could you?" Meshta wrung his hands. "The meeting was interrupted by the Security Patrol and they fled."

Gunrtok added, "We feared for a time that they would all be lost to us, but they eluded the Patrol in the forest. We heard from Grshluk shortly afterward. He had followed your friend until he entered Purgatory."

The Captain had holstered his weapon and stepped up beside Bennett. "How soon will we be able to move on this operation? Are your people ready to move?"

"We cannot say for certain," Meshta said. "Grshluk is waiting without the building to hear from your Eric."

Bennett was fidgeting still. "Yes, but was there any time frame involved? Does he know when…"

He was interrupted by a very loud roaring noise booming across the city. The ground shook. Bennett squatted, legs spread as the ground shook. Everyone else grabbed onto something to stabilize themselves.

"What in God's name was that?" Captain Anderson held a tent pole and looked around. "Do these people have artillery?"

After exchanging worried glances, Meshta and Gunrtok shook their heads. "No," Gunrtok spoke, "it is Klakmonidos. He is summoning his troops to fall back. We are running out of time."

Anderson looked at Bennett. "Klakmonidos? Do they mean Satan?" Bennett nodded.

Meshta said, "Yes, I believe that is the name you call him."

Rubbing his chin, the Captain looked from one to the other. "Anyone have any bright ideas about now? It might be a pretty good notion as it's about the right time to open up."

"No, sir." Bennett shrugged. "I guess we'll just have to go after the withdrawing demons and be on the lookout for the trap."

Meshta shook his head. "No, there will be no further dangers anywhere else in town. The trap will be coming from the Citadel. Klakmonidos has his weapon ready to fire down the length of the large Causeway."

Gunrtok nodded. "He plans to kill all your men with one blast. He needs as many of them there as possible."

"It is something to be avoided at all costs." Meshta looked at the Captain. "Your men should be safe from any attack except from the Citadel. Klakmonidos has ordered no more firing. You should proceed as slowly as possible."

"Yes, I agree." The Captain nodded. "Wainwright, we need to see if the men can take some alternate routes. Not all the troops, of course, but the majority must avoid that Causeway."

"You mean everyone except the final wave under the General?"

He shook his head. "No, not all of them. If Ironguts… er, General Strittmeier reaches the causeway with his troops and sees none of the forward squadrons, he will not be pleased." He grinned though tense. "And you know what happens when he is not pleased."

Bennett nodded. And gulped.

CHAPTER TWENTY

Augie's plan was quite simple.

And also quite impossible. Even with extended time – if that was what was happening here – there was simply not enough time to release every soul in Purgatory.

"No, no, no!" Augie slapped his fist into his palm. "It does not work that way at all, young man. Once we start releasing souls, someone is going to notice. Something will set off the alarm and the souls will awaken of their own volition. Can you imagine the million souls in one cell being held back by a single demon? The onslaught will overwhelm. The souls will escape!"

Maybe he knew more about it than I did (probably true) but it seemed a little risky to me. After checking my ordnance, I was pretty sure I did not have enough to take out every demon from every cell we had passed. And that was assuming there was only one demon per cell.

I supposed I was going to have to hit them in the head with the butt of my rifle… but that might mean alarms would be sent telepathically. From what Augie was saying, that was now the least of our problems.

The least. And what was the most?

"The greatest problem I foresee is getting the souls convinced they are now free to leave." He nodded back toward his cell behind us. "If you will notice, my fellow cellmate had not budged in the time we were there. He remained in his harness." His head shook. "Usually, only the really obstinate fellows, those of us who escape repeatedly, are sent to the lower levels; treated to intense forms of torture. Usually, when the torture ceases, reality can be glimpsed again and another escape effected. Sadly, he was not so quick to rouse."

I glanced around and looked at the women. "So, is the purpose of the exercise to disrupt the place, chase the spirits out, or what? If we shut the place down and the spirits stay put, are we sunk?"

"If you are asking if the plan can succeed without the spirits actually exiting…" He nodded. "I am certain of it."

"And we don't have to worry about the demons sending their warnings?"

"No. At the first disruption, an alarm should be sent."

"All right, then." I unshouldered my rifle. "Ladies, you are…"

Elizabeth backed away. "I am not going to shoot anyone!"

"Neither am I." I grinned. "And I am not giving you the rifle. I doubt you could carry it for very long, if at all." I took off my helmet. "But I think you can carry this." I held it out for her.

She took it tentatively and I was glad to see it did not simply pass through her hands. I still don't understand the first thing about ghosts.

"You want me to wear this?"

"Not at all. I want you to smash the machine the demons are using to control the torture chambers."

The tension fell from her face and she smiled, nodding. Veronica stepped forward eagerly. "And what do you have for me?"

Pulling my canteen off my belt, I passed it over. It was the only other good bludgeoning tool I had. "This should work. Just push the demon aside and smash the control board."

"The what?" Elizabeth was turning the helmet in her hands, staring at the wires.

"The podium the demons are standing at. Just hit it really hard with that thing and it should disable the system." I chuckled. "Unless they have much better engineering than we have. Which I doubt."

Augie stepped forward. "Are we ready?"

Nodding I started back up the corridor. "One thing. I think we should ignore the really small rooms and just go for the really crowded ones."

I looked around. Everyone nodded.

Before going too far, Elizabeth said, "Maybe we should try one or two of the smaller rooms first. You know, to sort of practice on?"

It was a good idea.

And it worked like a charm.

In the first room, Veronica shoved the demon aside and brought the canteen down in a shower of sparks. The dazed demon just lay on the floor where he fell.

Further along, in the next room, Elizabeth pushed the demon away and brought the helmet down in another rewarding shower of electrical distress. She smiled, pleased at her mayhem.

This demon, however, was not going to take this lying down. He got up and charged her. Unflustered, she caught the fellow's head in a roundhouse swing, the helmet connecting in a very satisfying "thonk".

She grinned at the helmet and then at us. "It works as good as a frying pan."

It made we wonder about further adventures she might have had in her life but there was no time to query her further.

"Okay, people." I looked around at the grinning trio of souls. "Girls, you bop and bash as many as you can. Augie, you get in there and roust the awakened souls. Let's move as quickly as possible as we have a lot of ground to cover." I nodded to each. "I'll meet you all back at the exit and don't be slackadaisical!"

We trotted along the corridor, Veronica in the lead, passing quite a few smaller rooms before she paused and bolted into one. Elizabeth and I kept running. Soon, she angled for the next door and I continued alone.

When I arrived at the following cell, I was wondering why the alarm had not been raised. Perhaps it only went back to "central" wherever that was, but I should have thought the demons in the cells further along were not prepared to try and stop us.

Maybe they were still thinking it was some sort of an isolated problem. But if there were problems later, I would worry about it then. For now, I was entering the cell.

A demon was "busy" staring at the control monitor. Bumping him to the side, I raised my rifle and brought it down on the panel. A rewarding display greeted the physical impact.

The demon did not react to the intrusion. He didn't fall but he did not attack me either. He just stood there, practically lost. Much like minor functionaries everywhere, I assume. Perhaps he was too bored to even notice what was happening.

Before I reached the doorway, Augie rushed into the cell shouting at the spirits. "You are free, children of God, free! Praise God and arise from…"

Not having the time to stay for the remainder of the sermon, I raced toward the next cell to be freed. Veronica came grinning out of a cell as I passed.

"I haven't had this much fun since high school!"

"You go, girl!"

And she did. She was certainly not being slackadaisical.

Me neither. I rushed into the next cell.

CHAPTER TWENTY-ONE

Back at the entrance, Bennett was still having troubles. Mainly, it dealt with not having anyone to coordinate with but I had both my hands a little too full to get the message to him at that moment.

"Come on! Try harder, concentrate!"

"It is very difficult, Bennett." Meshta shook his head, pointing at the large piece of paper on the table. "We have nothing like this… this 'map' thing in our world. And I am having a little trouble attempting to visualize the street layouts in the manner you describe."

"But don't you have friends you're in contact with?"

Meshta's glance spoke volumes. "Yes, but trying to coordinate seventy different views of the streets from various rooftops is not something I am used to. If I had any sort of previous training with something like…"

Bennett had raised a hand. "Okay, okay, I get you. It's just that I'm getting a little worried about the timing." He glanced at the portal back to Earth. "I'm pretty sure that as soon as old Ironguts finishes skewering the Major, the next wave will come pouring through And I would prefer to be out of this general vicinity." He shook his head. "Otherwise the General will probably force us all to follow along with him."

"Us, too?" Gunrtok looked from Bennett to Meshta.

Bennett slapped his own head. "Damn! Forget dragging us along with him, if the General sees the two of you, I'll be shot on the spot as a traitor for dealing with the enemy."

"Then perhaps we should hurry." Meshta bent over the map again.

Shortly, the rough sketched lines showed Bennett everything he needed to know. "Sir!" Bennett looked up from the crude map spread out on the table. "I think we have something."

Anderson spoke a short message into the phone, signaled to Wong and they both came over, the Captain holding the radio headset pressed against his chest. "What have you got?"

Bennett nodded to Meshta who pointed to the map and explained.

"There are no completely cleared parallel roads to the Causeway but several that mirror it for a while. If your men could take this route," he drew his finger along the map, "and others follow this one, there might be a chance."

"Son, are these to scale?"

Meshta looked at Bennett and shrugged.

Bennett took over. "Pretty much, sir. And as narrow as some of these are we will not be able to get all our forces through there in any fashion but single file."

The Captain grunted. "Don't know that I'd want to bring them all that way anyway, son. If there were no troops appearing along the Causeway, following them bastards in their phony retreat, they would know we smelled the trap." He rapped his knuckles on the table. "Serjeant, direct a third of our units each along both of these corridors and send the final third out onto the Causeway to join the final wave under the General. But tell them to advance very, very slowly. Tell them there may be landmines or something. Anything to keep them from advancing too rapidly." He handed the phone to the Serjeant.

Wong nodded and turned as he lifted the radio headset to his face.

"Sir?" Bennett was worried. "That many men on the Causeway?"

"Can't be helped, soldier. If we sent less, the enemy would know we were up to something. If we move slow enough and remain visible to them, hopefully we can drag this out until your friend can pull the rabbit out of the hat." He grunted. "Hopefully, the General will not smell a rat. Hopefully he won't head count as they are advancing." He turned to Meshta. "Any word from your friend yet?"

"One moment…" His attention was drawn elsewhere a moment before he shook his head. "Nothing yet. Grshluk is still waiting outside Purgatory for some news."

Anderson stared at Bennett. "All we can do is wait." He nodded. "And pray."

Bennett laughed. "Sir, are you ordering us to pray in Hell?"

He laughed and nodded. "Yes, soldier, I most strenuously am."

CHAPTER TWENTY-TWO

Moving up through the bowels of Purgatory was a blur. Enter a room, incapacitate the demon operator and smash the machine. Whether or not the spirits budged was not my concern; I left that chore up to Augie.

With three of us doing the clean-up, there was a little confusion. Some cells I entered to find the guard rubbing his head and the control panel a smoking ruin. That wasn't too much of a bother as I could just backtrack and head to the next one.

When we got farther along, among the larger cells with many more souls being held, the work got a little trickier. Apparently, since there were so many more prisoners to look after, the fellows were rotated in shifts or something. The demons were more likely to react. Lower down, the guards seemed to be dazed when I entered. Higher up, they seemed to notice my presence.

I first noticed this about the level when the temperature was growing a little warm. I had just finished one cell and re-entered the corridor to head for the next when I heard a scream.

It sounded like Veronica. Turning back, I headed for the sounds of a scuffle. It was in the next cell back down the corridor.

The demon guard had Veronica in a bear hug and she struggled to get free.

When the fellow saw me enter, he threw her aside and came at me. I raised the rifle and pulled the trigger, holding it steady, waiting for the thing to fire. He reached out and grabbed the barrel just as the chemical reaction completed and it took him full in the face. He dropped like a bag of rocks.

I rushed over to Veronica to see if she was all right but she waved me off.

"The control panel! Smash it!"

Raising the butt of my rifle, I brought it down in a satisfying shower of sparks before turning back to her. She was already on her feet again and, though a little ruffled, picked up the canteen where it had fallen and motioned to the corridor.

Outside, she looked around and caught Elizabeth coming out of another cell. She waved her over.

"What's happened?" Elizabeth said. "You two don't look so good."

Veronica explained what happened.

"Oh, brother!" She hefted the helmet. It had several dings on it. "I guess I'm going to have to get rough with these guys." She smacked her hand with the headgear. "No more missus nice guy from here on."

Veronica nodded. "That's right. We have to hit the guy before we attack the panels. And when you hit them," she grinned, "hit them hard!"

Grinning, Elizabeth nodded and headed up the corridor.

I called after her, "If there's any problem, just scream."

She waved without turning.

Back to the other woman, I said, "Are you sure you're okay?"

"Right as rain." She hefted the canteen. "I wish this was a bit heavier…"

I reached for my belt. "You want a knife?" I undid the snap on my blade.

She drew back in distaste. "No, way too messy."

"You want the rifle?"

"No, too heavy." She sighed. "I'll just have to swing harder, I suppose."

"Good girl." I nodded. "And if there's any more trouble, remember: I'm no more than two doors away. Just scream."

She grinned. "You don't have to worry about that."

We got back to it.

From here onward the doors got further apart. Not only were the demons guards here more alert, the word had seem to be getting around that some freaks were running loose in the place.

Most of the guards were still at work on the control panels but they seemed to be listening for any intruders. Some of the fellows looked around when I entered and I had to shoot them rather than try anything fancy.

Every few rooms, there would be a scream and I would have to rescue either one of the girls. In one room it got especially messy when the demon holding Elizabeth did not simply throw her to the side as the others had.

"Shoot him! Shoot him!" Elizabeth's voice was strained trying to talk around the grip the fellow had on her throat.

But I couldn't shoot. With a normal rifle, at that range, it would have been easy but with the delay… who knows who would be in the sights if the guy moved. I snapped the catch on my blade and pulled it out, letting go of the rifle.

The guy kept Elizabeth between me and him and we circled around a couple of times, me looking for an opening while he kept the shield between us.

Not seeing any other way to end this any quicker, I rushed him with the knife out to the side. Basically I simply hugged Elizabeth and swung the blade around her. It connected with the fellow's back and he released his hold on his human shield.

Moving Elizabeth out of the way, just in time, the guy charged me. Unarmed, it ended rather quickly. I parried to the right, switched hands on the blade and drove it into his throat from the left. He went down still trying to grab ahold of me but went down all the same.

Stepping back to get my rifle, I saw Elizabeth standing by the door half-turned away, covering her face. Probably the best thing for her.

I raised the weapon and smashed the control panel, thankful that Veronica had not needed any help during this little excursion.

By the door, I stopped and patted Elizabeth's shoulder. "You okay? It's over now."

She peeked at me and shook her head. "Your uniform… it's such a mess!"

Looking down, I could see what she meant. There was a lot of blood on it. Fortunately, it was none of my own.

We got moving into the corridor again.

At the next doorway, Elizabeth paused, took a couple of deep breaths, raised the helmet and raced into the room. A very sharp "bonk!" followed, and the accompanying sound of something large hitting the floor.

She seemed to have recovered nicely. I moved on to the next cell.

So it went for I don't know how long. The trio of us racing along, creating mayhem and only twice more did I have to answer any alarms for assistance.

Somewhere in here I got to wondering how it was going with Augie. I had no idea if there were reinforcements somewhere in the bowels of the structure, some doorway we had missed leading to the guards' break room or something, or if Augie was just taking his time.

By this time, the temperatures were getting quite warm.

After leaving a very large cell, I entered the corridor to hear a noise coming from the bowels of the structure. Stopping, I cocked my ear. The sound was getting closer. I raised my rifle, sweaty palms getting a good grip, and waited.

The wait was not too long and I relaxed when I saw the stream of souls start coming past. A few at first but very quickly growing in number. I went along with them, upward.

At a cell just ahead, Elizabeth came out of the doorway to see the rushing crowds. She gave a war-whoop and raced to the next door.

I followed and continued past hers to the next cell.

As I entered, the guard turned, eyes wide. He crouched a bit and looked wildly from one side to the other. Before I could advance further into the room, he raced past me, panic-stricken. I smashed the panel and went along to the next cell.

The guard in this room had already fled. I smashed the box and returned to the hallway.

Ahead, I saw Veronica coming out of another cell. She was laughing and shaking her head. When she saw me, she said, "It's getting easier now!" I gave her the thumbs up before she headed upward.

Looking back down the corridor, I could see the flow of spirits was increasing. I had no idea what Augie was doing down there, but it was working like a charm. Perhaps once the flood had started it increased geometrically, the holding areas collapsing like dominoes.

I shook my head and continued to the next room.

By the time I got to the large room near the beginning where the volcano could be seen in the distance, it was apparent the spirits were leaving the room before I even got there. Many were still stuck in the flashes and lightning bolts but quite a few were passing straight through that confusion and leaving.

I smashed the box anyway, to help the rest of the souls to get the message, and back to the corridor. It was now like rush hour and the departing souls were thick. Their passage buffeted me as I continued upward.

CHAPTER TWENTY-THREE

While the two girls and I were trying to get the hell out of Purgatory, Bennett was launched into a little Purgatory of his own.

Captain Anderson set down the radio. "Well, boys. It's time to move!"

Bennett blanched. "Now, sir? But we haven't heard from Patterson!"

Chuckling, the Captain held out the receiver. "Fine, soldier. Do you want to explain that to the General? I'm certainly not going to do it."

From blanched, Bennett faded to ashen. "No, sir! You mean the final wave is beginning?"

"That's right, son. It's out of our hands, now." He turned to Wong. "Serjeant, get the word out that the final push is beginning and the last of the troops are coming in. Time to begin the push to the Citadel. All the units should head to their pre-assigned positions." Using the rudimentary map the demons had sketched out, various units had been directed how to move into the eastern or western corridor paralleling the Causeway. Well, all except for those guys who were going into the danger zone.

"Right, sir!" He turned to the radio and began the announcement.

"But, sir, what are we to…"

Anderson held up his hand. "Relax, Bennett. We have already done what we could do and the units have their assignments. Only a third are taking to the Causeway to be joined by the final wave and the rest are taking to the side streets." He clapped his hand on Bennett's shoulder. "And, you, son, are going to lead the eastern flank. That way, when – and if – your partner contacts us we will know better what to do."

"Yes, sir. But how am I to do that? All the squad leaders outrank me."

The Captain grinned. "Because I'll be going with you. You think I want to be the only one standing around here when the General arrives?" He turned to the two demons. "Since Wong is heading up the western flank he'll need one of you with him."

Meshta discussed it with his friend a moment before nodding. "Gunrtok will accompany your Serjeant and I will go with you and friend Bennett."

"Good." The Captain signaled to Wong, who nodded and got off the radio. "Serjeant, you've got a guide to the western corridor. You know what to do?"

Wong saluted smartly and signaled to his demon guide.

"Wait!" Bennett raised his hands. "Just a moment, here. Don't you think we should have some sort of insignia or something for these fellows so none of our troops thinks they're enemy infiltrators of something?"

"Serjeant?" Anderson turned to his aide. "You got anything for these fellows?"

Wong turned to rummage through some equipment a moment before turning back with two helmets and armbands blazoned with red crosses. "Sir, will these do?"

He waved him forward. "Better than nothing, I suppose." He took one and handed it to Meshta. "Will these things fit you?"

The demon's head was a little smaller than the helmet was intended for but, by tightening the chin strap, it held in place pretty good. The Captain nodded. "Pretty good" was, as in many cases, good enough.

"All right, boys. If you two could lead us to the causeway by the fastest route? I really don't want to be in this position when the General comes through."

Meshta nodded to his partner. "Certainly! Follow us."

Wong took off after Gunrtok. Meshta led the other way with Bennett and Captain Anderson in close pursuit.

Bennett was muttering, "Eric, where the hell are you, old boy? It's getting later than you think."

CHAPTER TWENTY-FOUR

By the time I was done with my last cell, Elizabeth was waiting at the edge of the corridor leading to the exit. In a couple of moments we were joined by Veronica.

I had to raise my voice over the sound of the rushing souls. "Any sign of Augie?"

Elizabeth shook her head. Veronica craned her neck to peer along the corridor. Many of the souls were practically transparent – don't ask me why – and some were fairly solid in appearance. Seeing through and/or around them was fairly easy even with so many coursing through the small space.

Veronica shook her head. "No sign of him yet."

"We can wait a bit." I leaned against the wall. "Whew! That was rough."

"I thought it went fairly easy," Veronica said and Elizabeth nodded her agreement. "I believe we got through the entire place in record time."

"Yeah, that part went well enough," I said, though I wondered what record she was referring to, "but it was the actual killing. I'm trained as a soldier, ma'am, not an assassin. Or a murderer."

"Oh, I see. I hadn't considered that part of it. I suppose you could see a priest or something and confess…" She smirked.

Elizabeth laughed. "Yes, one should be along in just a little while."

"Maybe so. It wasn't so bad with the ones that attacked us…" I sighed. "Now if we only knew where Augie was…"

"It seems a little close in here," Elizabeth said, "and we seem to be blocking the way somewhat. Perhaps we should wait without?"

"Outside? Sure!" I led the way.

In the entry vestibule, light shone in through the door that was being held open by the constant stream of exiting spirits. I stepped out and to the right to allow room for the ladies.

"There you are!"

The voice was behind me and I whipped around, raising my rifle but stopped short when I saw it was Grshluk and some friends. A couple I think I recognized from the little club meeting we held in the barn what seemed like several weeks ago.

"Grshluk! Don't startle me like that! I almost shot you!"

"Sorry, friend. We followed you through the woods. We were not certain what sort of insanity you were involved in." He glanced at his companions. "It is a shame we could not stay in contact with you as we do with each other." He shrugged. "As we could not tell what adventure you were involved in, we held back some distance. And when you entered into this evil place, we worried some.

"Still, we waited to see what might come of it. When we saw the rush of beings come out of the place we realized what you were up to." He chuckled. "Quite a brilliant move on your part, I must say."

I grinned. "Oh, yeah, but I can't take credit for it. It was Veronica here that had the idea." I turned and smiled at her. "Grshluk, this is Veronica, one of the spirits trying to get out of here." Grshluk bowed his head toward her. "And this is Elizabeth, Veronica's friend who helped us."

Grshluk nodded to her as well. "So, are we ready to attack the Citadel?"

I glanced back inside. Souls were still pouring out the door. "We're still waiting for one more. Saint Augie is around here someplace."

Veronica turned to her friend. "Imagine. A friendly demon." They smiled at Grshluk.

He bowed a little deeper. "At your service."

At this moment Saint Augustine exited the building with the last of the souls.

"Augie! How did it go!"

The Saint stopped at the doorframe and leaned on it with a sigh. "Not as well as I had hoped. So many of the tormented souls must still truly believe they belong here. They chose to remain."

Rubbing his shoulder, Veronica consoled him. "Perhaps they feared it was some sort of trap."

He nodded wearily. "Perhaps. And they feared further torments. I believe I released a vast majority of them." He shook his head. "I pray that I did." He sighed. "I fear that so many of them may have been trapped here through some teachings of mine these many long years ago." He blinked his eyes and seemed to look around for the first time, spotting Grshluk and friends. He did not recoil. "And who are these?"

"Saint Augustine, this is my friend Grshluk and some of his companions that are helping us."

"Imagine. Angels in demon clothing!"

Grshluk began moving down the steps. "Yes, but we should be moving along. I fear that Klakmonidos will use the weapon while we continue engaged in such friendly banter." He waved everyone forward. "It is a short distance now."

From the entry landing at Purgatory, we could see the path along the river leading to another set of steps leading up to the side entrance of the main portico of the Citadel. If Klakmonidos came out to the front edge of the building, he would be able to see them easily. Fortunately, the monster was not visible.

I wondered at the time what could be going on in the place. Surely the alarm had been raised there by now about the escapees from Purgatory. If Augie was right about the souls being used as the power source for Satan's big weapon, I wonder if there was still any major danger to our troops. Since I was not seeing any signs of panic around the Citadel, I had the sinking feeling that there might have been more to the story than Augie knew.

There was nothing I could do about that now, though.

Looking to the right was another smaller set of steps leading to an entrance further back than the large public opening of the Citadel. I thought that should be the perfect place to enter the monster's lair.

Scanning to the left, I looked out over the hodge-podge of the city wondering how the troops were getting along and where the heck Bennett was at the moment.

Then I remembered I had a method of discovery to hand.

"Wait! Grshluk!" I ran down the steps to where he was. "How about your friends? Did they make contact with Bennett?"

"Oh, yes." He grinned. "Two of our comrades are with your troops now. They are advancing on the Citadel as we speak."

My eyes widened. "But the trap…!?"

He raised a hand to stop me. "Do not fear. Bennett says that his leader has split the troops…"

"General Ironguts?!"

"No, I believe it was an Anderson person." Eric nodded. "Only a small portion of the troops are advancing along the Causeway. The remainders have been split between two other avenues of advance each with one of my associates. I believe it effectively neutralizes what Klakmonidos was planning."

"And I hoped what we had done in Purgatory had neutralized the weapon as well but I'm not seeing any evidence of it… no scurrying demons over at the Citadel, no panic, no wailing."

"Perhaps," Grshluk said, "there was more to his plan than we know. But, alas, it is too late to alter what we have already set in motion. We must just keep moving."

"Yes. Let's get moving!"

CHAPTER TWENTY-FIVE

Bennett craned his neck down an alley as they advanced quietly down the side street. He could see demons backing slowly down the Causeway toward the Citadel.

"They're still falling back but their numbers are thinning. I'm afraid most of them have gathered in the Citadel. That must mean that Satan – or whatever his name is – is about to unleash his weapon."

Meshta said, "Gunrtok says most of the men in the other group are on the side street opposite us. It is not as straight a road as the Causeway but they are making as good a time as we."

Captain Anderson stopped. "I can't be sure where the latest wave is but I should imagine they'd be on the Causeway by now, judging from the steady withdrawal of the enemy."

Meshta nodded. "Yes, some observers along the route state that your General has begun the march along the far end of the Causeway. Apparently your warning about the supposed dangers…"

"Land-mines?"

"Yes, just that. It keeps their advancement slow but they are advancing steadily.

The Captain shook his head. "I wish I had sent fewer men to that route. With the reinforcements of the next wave it is going to be a sizeable force. If anything goes wrong, we're going to lose a lot more than I had counted on."

"It couldn't be helped, sir." Bennett looked at Meshta. "If we don't hear from Eric, all of us may be lost, regardless."

"True." The Captain looked in the direction of the Citadel. "We need to get ourselves as near the Citadel as possible so we can be in a position to attack when your friends are ready. Or to support the troops on the Causeway if we don't hear from them." He turned to Meshta. "Any word on their position yet?"

He shook his head, the helmet swiveling a little behind the motion of his head. "I have heard nothing yet."

"All right." Anderson said. He grinned at Bennett. "What surprises me is that the General has not ignored the chatter about the landmines. With the demons retreating along the Causeway one would think they might accidentally set off a couple."

Bennett shrugged. "Maybe he just figures the demons can avoid them psychically or something."

"Hrmph! Probably so! All right, we keep moving and get as close to the Citadel as we can until we do hear something." He looked at Bennett. "Fortunately, with these friends of yours, we can stay in contact with the others even without radio."

"Yes." Bennett signaled to the rest of the troop and they began moving forward again.

A few moments later, Meshta began bouncing up and down. He rushed over the Bennett and tugged his sleeve.

He stopped and saw the agitation on the demon. "What is it?"

"I have heard from Grshluk. Your friend is out of Purgatory now. He says they are planning on approaching the Citadel from the side. There's an entrance there."

"Great!" He ran forward to deliver the news to the Captain.

"Well, that's good news." The Captain looked around. "Only problem I have at the present is in figuring out how much further we have to go? I can't tell how far it is to the Citadel with all these buildings around."

Meshta said, "It is not far, now. We should be there in a matter of minutes."

"Then let's get moving! I'd hate to be late for this party."

While Meshta and Bennett moved ahead along the cluttered street, climbing over piles of rubble and collapsed buildings, Captain Anderson remained to wave the troops past.

With a little luck, maybe all their plans wouldn't be shot to hell.

In a manner of speaking.

CHAPTER TWENTY-SIX

As we made our way across the clearing heading for the Citadel, I noticed what seemed to be a cloud forming overhead. Glancing up, I noticed it seemed to be a roiling mass sort of like those time-lapse films of thunder-clouds forming.

Augie was next to me and he laughed. "A little confused, my friend?"

"Well, yeah. What's happening overhead? Is Klakmonidos up to something we don't know about?"

"No, those are the spirits freed from Purgatory. Some desire revenge, some are just curious, but they all have some stake in what transpires here. I think they may be of some help."

I wasn't sure what a cloud of mist was going to be able to do but I recalled the buffeting they created in the corridor as we escaped. They may not be very solid, individually, but en masse they might be formidable.

"Okay, Augie. I'll leave the spiritual hocus-pocus to you."

He just chuckled.

We reached the stairway ascending to the side of the Citadel, unbroken but for the one small door at the head of the stair. It was a bit wider than the stair leading to Purgatory and we managed two abreast all the way to the top.

On the platform before the door, I stopped and turned to Grshluk. "What sort of entrance is this? Are there going to be a lot of people around inside?"

"I believe this is the service entrance for the Purgatory operations. Supplies and such are taken from here to Purgatory and maintenance staff." He shrugged. "I have no idea if there are people currently near this entrance."

"Okay. We'll just have to be ready for anything." I readied the rifle and grabbed the handle. It wouldn't budge. Pressing harder, I jerked it up and down but got nothing. "Damn! It's sealed tight. What do we do now? Is there any other entrance?"

"Only around the front." Grshluk pointed. "By the Causeway."

Gritting my teeth, I bit back a curse. There were women present after all, even if only in spirit form. "How do we get to the front of the building?"

"I believe there is a path along the river."

"Yeah, I remember seeing that. It's not very wide though."

Grshluk smiled. "Yes, it is small. Which means we will have to advance single file."

Signaling everyone to head back down, I shouldered my weapon and worried.

"I shouldn't worry," Grshluk said behind me. "I don't believe anyone will be looking for us here. They are all too busy elsewhere."

"I certainly hope you're right."

Augie chuckled and glance over his shoulder at me. "I would not be certain about that, friend. I believe Satan knows we are coming even without being told."

"Oh, great!" It was what I had figured but it could've remained a minor bother until it was just laid bare like that.

Augie suddenly stopped and looked upward. "Oh, dear."

Looking up, I tried to see what the trouble was. Did Klakmonidos have an air force we didn't know about? Space ships? What? Then I noticed the cloud overhead had stretched outward, a long strand stretched out over the city, toward where the entry portal was. Were they trying to get back to Earth?

"What's the problem, Augie? Are they leaving?"

He shook his head. "No, they are being drawn away." He motioned with his hands and several spirits came down toward him. I didn't hear any words exchanged but they seemed to be communicating.

The rest of the group had stopped when we stopped and were looking as puzzled as I must have. Elizabeth came back up a couple of steps and took my arm.

"Most of them are waiting to see Satan get his butt kicked but many are being led astray."

"I thought maybe they were just trying to get back to Earth or something."

She shook her head. "No, there is a force there… a powerful attractive force…"

It hit me. "It's the generator that Satan is using to hold the portal open. I forgot about that! And I think he was using the souls in Purgatory to power it."

She shook her head. "No, it is nothing here. It is something drawing them from the other side."

My earlier thought seemed to have been correct. "Then they just want to get back to Earth." I wondered how people would feel with several million new hosts inhabiting the place. But there was more.

"No, it is not their personal desires drawing them there, it is a machine…"

"That's the gen-…"

"No, not from here. It is over *there*!" She locked on my eyes. "Someone *over there* is drawing them back."

Then I remembered all the parabolic dishes and the huge generators surrounding the entrance in St. Peter's square. It seemed like far too much power than they would need to power the lights and radio equipment. Satan may have held the portal open for a time but now it was our people keeping it open.

Yeah, with our predilection for "scientific study" I should imagine a whole bunch of countries would like to keep the portal open to study a parallel universe. Just imagine how much easier it would be to travel to other worlds and strip them of their resources. It would be far more cost-effective than space travel.

But the situation was a little too cockamamie for me to comprehend. If Satan, Klakmonidos, whoever, had used the power of the souls to hold the gate open and it was now being held open from our side, why would it pull the souls over there? I'm not much up on physics and such but it made no sense.

Elizabeth looked worried. "Maybe someone could go and try to disable the generators?"

What a mess! If the spirits were being pulled away, they couldn't help us in our chore of combating Klakky. If the generators in St. Peter's were shut off – since there was no more power source on this side – the portal would simply close. We'd be trapped in Hell!

Here I was in the middle of a combat operation and was being hit with sixteen new crises all of which were somewhat above my pay grade. What the hell! I wasn't an officer! Where were they when you really needed one?

Officers! Of course! I seriously doubted any of this could not be happening without the knowledge – and cooperation – of one rather important General. Just another part of operations that was on a need-to-know basis and it now seemed that the troops on the ground had a very urgent need-to-know.

All that panic took place in my head in about the space of two seconds. A hand clapping on my shoulder brought me out of panic mode.

Augie looked a little grim. "The power field that is drawing them thither is so very similar to the ones that held them in bondage in Purgatory. From what Miss Elizabeth has said, I have the feeling that should that energy cease, you might find yourself trapped here. Is that correct?" I could only nod. "Very well. I know of a way to pull the spirits away from that distraction – or at least most of those so drawn – but it will place your and your friends in serious jeopardy. I think we must assist you in your mission first to repay you for releasing us but I fear we must be quick. These souls are weakened after years of torture."

I settled my rifle on my shoulder and glanced up. "How can you do that?"

He nodded sagely. "By taking them home. To Heaven."

"You can do that?" It took the guy centuries in Hell to figure it out.

He nodded again. "But when I do, we shall depart for good. So we must be quick."

"All right. Everyone, let's get moving!"

From here on, I ran. Down the stairs, over toward the river and up the narrow pathway leading to the Citadel. I didn't even bother to look around and make sure anyone was following me until I reached the stone steps leading up to the huge viewing platform that overlooked the Causeway.

From my location, I couldn't see either the Causeway or any of our fellows though I could hear the footsteps of their combat boots in the distance. Several demons were going up the wide stairway from the Causeway up into the Citadel but none glanced in my direction.

Turning around, I was gratified to see the group had kept up with me, or at least caught up to me while I was sight-seeing. Grshluk and his friends were panting a bit but the spirits all seemed to be fit and, well, in good spirits. I suppose floating along at a fast pace was not much more of a strain than gliding along at a leisurely pace.

"Well, Grshluk. Can you get in touch with your friends so we can make a plan of what to do now?"

He panted a couple of times before replying. "Certainly."

I glanced at Augie. "And make sure it's something quick."

CHAPTER TWENTY-SEVEN

Captain Anderson worked his way through the troops up to where Bennett had stopped behind a huge pile of rubble. "We're stopping here?"

"Yes, sir." Bennett pointed ahead. "This road exits onto the Causeway just around that turn and it's only about twenty feet from there to the steps leading up to the Citadel."

Standing on tiptoe, the Captain surveyed the scene. Klakmonidos was pacing back and forth while demons scurried up from the Causeway and disappeared into the building. At the far right side of the platform sat a rather large cannon-looking affair resting on a cradle. Wires and cables draped from the weapon.

"Damn! That big, ugly guy must be Satan."

Bennett craned to see. "Yes, sir. Jeez! He's a big mutha, ain't he… uh, sir?"

Private Ferguson climbed a little on the rubble to get a look. "Whoa! That guy's been snorting some serious growth hormones or something!"

Anderson squatted down. "It would appear most of the demons have left the Causeway and I can hear our troops advancing. Any idea how far they've come?"

Bennett shook his head. "Sorry, sir, but I can't tell. Do you want me to send some eyes…"

"No, I don't want to do anything that might give away our position." He shook his head. "Why not just ask your friend?" He nodded toward Meshta.

Blushing, Bennett said, "Meshta, ask your friends how far our troops have advanced."

He nodded. "They are sending frequent updates. Right this moment, the advanced troops are nearing the halfway point of the Causeway."

Bennett glanced back toward the Citadel. "Damn! That means he's going to use the weapon any moment!"

"Not just yet, friend. There are still more troops entering onto the Causeway at the far end. Klakmonidos will wait until the last of them are in the range of the weapon."

The Captain interrupted. "Did you see that huge contraption up there?"

"Yes." Bennett nodded. "Do you suppose that's the weapon we've been warned about?"

Meshta nodded, looking from one to the other. "Yes, that is the instrument he plans to unleash on your people."

"Man! That's a big fucking gun!" Bennett shook his head. "More like a cannon!"

Anderson glanced around. "Wainwright, any chance you could get to that BFG?"

Bennett gulped. "Uh, not at present, sir. Maybe if we had some sort of diversion…"

"Hey!" Ferguson pointed to the right of the Citadel. "Isn't that Patterson over there?"

Anderson stood. "Where, son?"

"Over here, sir." Ferguson stepped aside and pointed again. "You can just see through the doorway in that gutted building."

Craning his neck to find the sweet spot, Anderson grunted. "Yes, Wainwright. There's your friend over there and he's got company."

Nodding, Bennett was at the Captain's shoulder gazing through the ruins of the building. "Yep, that's Eric and he's got Grshluk with him. I don't have a clue who those others are." He squinted a little. "Are those women?"

Anderson grinned and shook his head. "Only in Hell would a soldier bring the women-folk to a fire-fight." He clapped Bennett on the soldier. "Well, soldier. Can that be enough of a diversion for you?"

Turning to Meshta, Bennett said, "Can you tell them to rush the Citadel when we do?"

"Yes. They have just contacted us to find out what we can do now. There seems to be some urgency but there seems to not be enough time to explain at present."

Anderson nodded. "Fine by me. Personally, I've gotten tired of all this horseshit. Let's *do* something for God's sake!"

"Yes, sir."

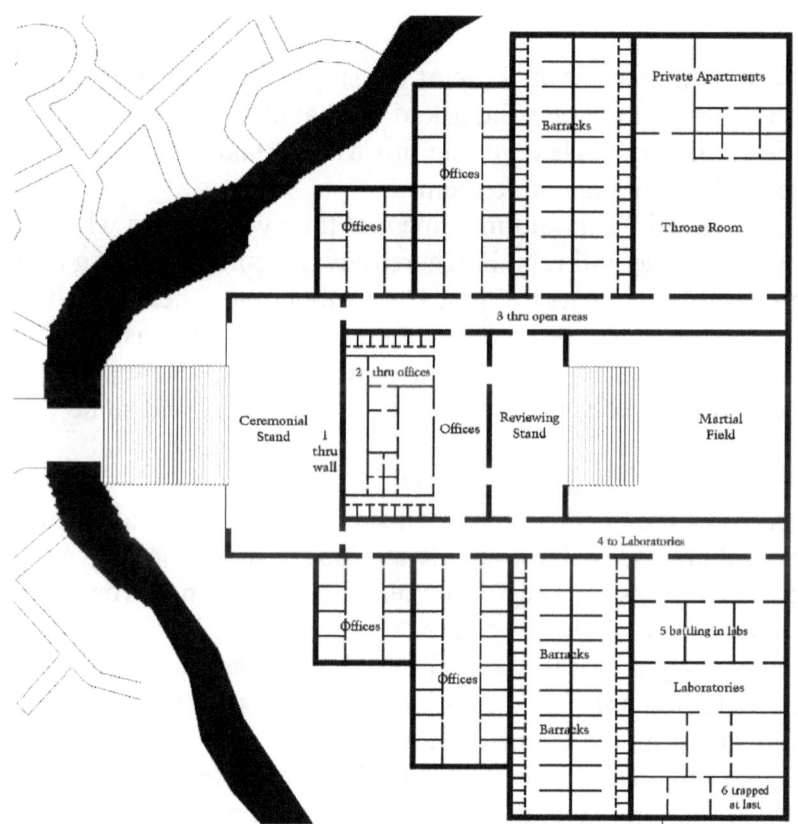

DETAIL OF THE CITADEL

CHAPTER TWENTY-EIGHT

We settled down at the base of the steps while Grshluk made contact. I turned to Augie and asked, "What about the souls still stuck in Purgatory? When you do this trick to take everyone to Heaven, what will happen to them?"

He shrugged. "I should imagine that they will remain where they are – just as some will remain where they are currently being drawn – even as the rest depart for their Heavenly home. There are always those who, for some reason or another, cannot tear themselves away from this plane. Either guilt or fear or regrets. I believe that is what ghosts in our world have been: spirits who felt they had some unfinished business."

"But what will happen to them?"

"Like ghosts, I believe they will stay as long as it takes them to work out their issues. They are always free to leave for Heaven whenever they desire. They will make their way home eventually." He nodded firmly. "This I believe."

I cannot say if that is correct or not but at least Augie seemed to think so. He probably knew a lot more about it than I and probably a lot more about it now than he did when he was a living Saint.

Grshluk tugged my sleeve. "Your friends are in place."

"Really?" I craned to see some sign of their presence. No such luck.

"They are hiding in a side street but I get the sense that they know where we are."

"Okay. So what's the plan?"

Grshluk described the situation from Bennett's point of view. None of the action on the Citadel's platform was visible from where we stood so I was happy to have some idea of what was happening.

"So, they want us to rush the Citadel at the same time? Or what?"

"Apparently," Grshluk struggled with some concepts, "we are to be some sort of 'diversionary tactic', whatever that is."

"Got it." I unshouldered my weapon. "Tell him I'm ready whenever he is."

Grshluk looked away. "One moment. We are trying to get the other group ready as well."

"What other group?"

"It would seem that one of our colleagues is with your Bennett and another is with another group on the far side of the Causeway."

"Oh, a triangulation, eh?" I grinned. "This should be fun!"

"Everyone is ready now."

Putting one foot on the steps, I nodded. "Give the word. Let's do this thing!"

He raised one finger, before nodding. "They are proceeding."

I raced up the stairs, screaming a battle cry as I went. It was gratifying to hear a couple of similar calls going up, coming closer, all converging on the heights at the Citadel.

Oh, crap! Just as my head came level with the platform, I saw this really huge demon – it had to have been Satan himself – coming toward me. Before I could bring my weapon to bear, he stopped and picked up the biggest rifle – more like a cannon – I had ever seen. He kicked the rack it had been sitting on to the side.

Up the main steps from street level, I saw Bennett rushing toward the gun before Klakky snatched it up. I flung myself to the side and braced my back against a pillar as I took aim.

Klakmonidos roared and waved the weapon in front of him, then took aim at the causeway. Bennett had dropped to the steps when Klakmonidos waved the weapon around and now was looking at me. I don't know what he expected me to do.

I fired at the big monster and I know I hit him but he didn't even flinch. Though not exactly sure about it, I think the bullet simply bounced off him. We were going to need some serious ordnance to bring this bad boy down and I looked at Bennett and shrugged.

Roaring again, Klakmonidos turned the weapon on the fellows rushing the platform from the far side. I held my breath, waiting for the vaporization to begin.

Nothing happened.

Klakky drew the weapon up and examined it, fiddling with a knob or adjustment before lowering it again to fire.

Again, nothing happened.

He leaned his head back and roared again, flinging the useless weapon to the side. It skittered across the platform to stop not five feet from me.

The unarmed monster turned to the legions of demons milling around on the platform and signaled to the invaders. He roared, "Kill them all!' And when they didn't move quickly enough, "KILL THEM ALL!!!"

Before the demons could move, I dashed to the weapon and snatched it up, moving quickly back over to the side to be out of the way. Bennett scrambled up the steps and dodged a demon as he made his way to me.

In the distance yelling could be heard as the troops at the far end of the Causeway raced toward the demons massing before the Citadel.

Pointing at the weapon, Bennett joined me. He had to yell over the rising noise level. "That thing doesn't work! Didn't you see Klakmonidos? It doesn't work!"

I grinned and tried hefting the weapon. It was heavy. "It didn't work for him because he didn't have the power connected."

"What?"

I turned to where Grshluk and Augustine stood on the stairs near the platform. "Augie! You guys ready?" I grinned at Bennett. "I hope this works."

Staggering a little under the weight, I advanced across the platform toward Satan.

Seeing my efforts, he laughed and roared again. "Stupid human! That weapon is useless!"

As he spoke, I felt a faint vibration coming from the machine. Presently it grew to a steady hum. I laughed and aimed the weapon. "Maybe it just won't work for you, Klakky!" I pulled the trigger.

The weapon kicked and I was pushed backward. It reminded me of a scene from a classic movie about a group of ghosthunters learning to fire their atomic-powered weapons. The bolt went to the side of Klakky, blasting a sizeable hole in the wall before wandering above his head and gravitating upward before I could release the trigger.

Klakmonidos roared and pounded his chest. I was beginning to wonder if we were going through an album of old movies because that reminded me of King Kong.

"Whoa!" Bennett jumped back. "That was pretty cool."

I yelled at Klakky above the noise. "Don't worry, I'll get you with the next one, big guy." I raised the weapon again as Klakky let loose with of a string of only what I could describe as a litany of demonic curse words. Before I could get it leveled on him, Klakmonidos noticed the hole blown in the wall by the blast and ducked through it. My next shot widened the previous hole and beyond to where Klakmonidos had disappeared.

"Damn! Missed!" I lowered the weapon again.

But Bennett was already giving chase, waving me forward. "Come on, Eric! We got him on the run!" He dove through the hole.

I hoped the big guy wasn't merely crouching beyond the hole or Bennett was *so* going to be toast. Still, I followed best I could while hampered with an eighty pound metal salami. Maneuvering the damned thing through the cockeyed opening was a bear but I wasn't about to set the thing down before climbing through.

The room beyond was strewn with rubble – thanks to yours truly – and there were several demons scattering for their lives but no sign of the big guy. The room looked like it could have been a mess hall. There were long tables arranged around the room. Once, I suppose they had been in some order and not strewn with rubble.

I spotted Bennett across the room.

"Where is he?"

Bennett shrugged. "I don't know. He was gone before I came through the wall."

Scanning, I could see a small hole high in the wall opposite, probably in line-of-sight with my first shot, and two doors. One to the left, one to the right. Figuring the fellow could not have shimmied up the wall and squeezed through the small hole I had made, he had to have gone through one of the two doors.

Both were big enough to accommodate his stature. So, did we split up or… Nah. Going empty-handed against this guy was definitely in the category of "very *bad* ideas".

I ran across the room toward Bennett. "Just pick a door and let's go! Time's a wastin'!"

The door to the right appeared to lead into a corridor while the one to the left seem to have more light coming in. Bennett pointed to the left. I steadied the weapon and advanced that direction while he fell in behind me.

We were big-game hunting, major league style.

CHAPTER TWENTY-NINE

I went through the doorway into what seemed to be an office. Desks were piled with piles of paper but the room was otherwise empty. I charged through the opposite doorway into a large well-lit area with Bennett on my heels.

"Do you see him?"

Bennett looked both ways the same as I and came up with the same result.

"Nothing! Which way did…"

At that moment a group of demons came out of a corridor to the left. Bennett swung his weapon but it was too late. He wasn't going to be able to get off a shot before they reached us.

I punched the trigger of the weapon and swung it toward the attackers. The first few on the right of the group simply vanished. The ones at the left broke off and dashed back into the corridor.

Rubble fell from the wall and ceiling where the power beam had cut a ragged swath.

I looked at Bennett.

He was hefting his rifle. "These things are useless in close quarters, huh?" He glanced around. "Let's try this way." He started to the doorway across the large room.

Struggling to get through the doorway with the large piece of equipment was a chore but I hurried to pull up next to Bennett. We were in a large area open to the sky. We looked down some steps to what appeared to be a small arena, maybe a combat practice area. The dirt looked undisturbed.

Bennett said, "Doesn't look like he's been that way. Surely we'd see his big ugly footprints."

We heard a crashing noise somewhere to the left. Turning that direction we followed down a corridor. Passing through a set of double doors, we stopped in our tracks and backed out quickly as stones and other objects slammed into the rapidly closing doors.

"How many did you see?" I asked.

"I couldn't tell, most were hunkered down behind the overturned tables." He paused a moment in recall. "There were four overturned tables and… and a couple of guys hiding behind what looked like an over-blown throne. I count three others."

"I saw five free-standing demons. And the four tables."

"Can that weapon take care of them all? I mean before we get shot?"

I nodded. "We may have to take it in a couple of tries. I learned to dance with the rifle but it was a lot lighter than this damned thing. I'll shoot one way and back out again." I braced myself. "If you'll get the doors?"

Bennett got to the doors and pulled the right one open at my signal. Stepping in quickly, I pressed the trigger, swept the room from the left and stepped back. Missiles slammed against the door, one large stone ricocheting off the closing door and just missing my kneecap.

Sweating, I nodded to Bennett. "That was close."

"Yeah. Ready to go again?"

I nodded and he opened the door again.

Planning to start from the middle of the room this time, I saw several of the fellows had moved over to the left, assuming I would start where I left off. So I gave the left another blasting.

When I jumped back this time, very few stones crashed against the door. It was a hopeful sign.

"One more time should do it," Bennett said, grinning.

"On my mark." And I went in again, gun blazing. I finished the sweep of the room and, though I saw tables and other paraphernalia were destroyed, there was no sign of any demons.

I stepped back through the door. "Damn! I think they escaped after the second volley."

"Yeah, probably moved to a backup position." He opened the door again and I raced through the room to the door opposite, taking up a position with my back to the wall adjacent to the closed door.

Grabbing the door handle, Bennett asked, "Same routine?"

"As long as it keeps working."

*****

While we were engaged in our leisurely tour of the Citadel with the Big Guy himself, there was a major shit-storm brewing back at the portal. Bennett and I were both a little busy to even notice the battle going on between the demons and our forces at the base of the steps on the Causeway. The major shit-storm was happening just a little bit further away.

At the opposite end of the Causeway, the General had completed a rather short fact-finding mission of his on as to why certain conditions of the engagement seem to have been, well, overlooked.

"Major!" The General barked in the officer's face. "Am I to understand that you have intentionally contravened my explicit orders?"

"Yes, sir. That is correct." The Major didn't flinch.

"Then your career is over, sir!" The General did not remove his eyes from the Major. "Serjeant! Have this man put into chains immediately!" Rearranging his cap, the General finally turned from the victim and marched toward the portal, muttering, "We'll see who else is involved in this mutiny."

The Serjeant and the Major exchanged glances. "Sir, I don't know what to say. I never seen the man go off like that..."

"Don't worry about it soldier. Just follow your orders."

"Well, yeah, sure... " He shrugged. "Any idea where I'm gonna find any chains?"

The Major grinned. "I'm sure we can figure something out." The pair followed the General back toward the portal.

There was no one at the HQ tent. Regardless, the General was yelling for someone there to come to his assistance. Unfortunately, all the troops were engaged in the advance on the Citadel. Screaming for *anyone* to come help, the General grabbed the corner pole of the tent and ripped it out of the ground. The tent settled slowly over the table and equipment piled below.

After kicking over a box or two, the General snapped the pole in two over his knee and marched off back toward the Causeway, in evident disgust. He did not even notice the wide-eyed Serjeant leading the arrested Major past the scene of the tantrum.

"Sir, did you see…"

The Major stopped him with a glance. "No, soldier, I did not see anything. And neither did you, got it?"

"Yes, sir!"
The prisoner preceded his jailor back to the surface.

As Major Hopkins was helping the Serjeant find some make-do chains back in sunny St. Peter's Square and Ironguts Strittmeier strode purposefully along the Causeway on another fact-finding mission, Bennett and I were still involved in tracking the chief demon through his lair.

The next room brought the same three-step attack as the previous room before it was cleared out and we entered unopposed.

Looking around this room – once you discounted all the rubble and mayhem we had caused – it looked like this was the private apartment of the big guy. The doors were opened and the rooms were empty. Including the emperor-sized bed.

Where had the guys got to?

"Over here." Bennett drew my attention to the side wall. Apparently I had punched a hole through that wall with one of the shots and the hole was not visible from our vantage. Probably because of the wardrobe that had fallen over.

I motioned to him. "Take a peek, Bennett. See which way we should go."

"Me?" He grinned. "You too valuable to risk?"

"No but it would be a little harder maneuvering with this." I hefted the BFG.

He shrugged and poked his head through. After looking to the left, he peeked again toward the right. "It's a small room but it's all clear."

"Yeah, right!" We entered the small room and Bennett peeked out that door.

"Looks like a barracks. There's a lot of really small rooms down both sides. Whatcha wanna do?"

I rearranged my grip, wiping off my sweaty palms on my trousers. "Do we really want to deal with a lot of small rooms? Let's go back the way we came. We're after the big guy not all his distractions."

"Sounds good," his grin got wider. "You got it!"

Back through the throne room, we paused to check out the corridor. I looked to the left and saw only a dead end. Since Bennett did not scream in panic, I assumed there were no bad guys coming up from the right. Still, I emerged into the passage cautiously.

Sticking my head out quickly, I glanced left and caught a movement. A very large leg disappeared through a doorway a few yards away.

"There he is!" And I was back in the chase hoping that, once again, Bennett would be watching my back. I hauled ass. Turning the corner, I saw that it was a room with small openings along its length.

I paused on entering the room and Bennett collided with my back, knocking me several feet ahead. I had the weapon raised and ready, scanning for a sign of Klakmonidos. I could not see any other exit but I didn't see the big guy either.

Bennett was a dozen steps behind when I turned and saw Klakky heading for the door. Where and how he had hidden was beyond me but I had time for one shot.

"Duck!" I yelled and pulled the trigger.

An upper corner of the doorway crumbled into ruins but I think I missed my target.

Bennett rose slowly from his crouch rubbing the side of his head. "Man, you almost took my ear off. Take it easy next time."

I ran past toward the wrecked doorway. "Then keep out of the way. I can't shoot him through you."

"Okay! Okay! Sheesh!"

Back into the corridor, I caught sight of the Big Guy on my left and set off in pursuit. As I neared the cross-passage he had taken, I slowed. There seemed to be a brighter orange glow ahead. Bennett caught up to me.

I shook my head. "It's almost like he's leading us on."

"Could just be your imagination." He chuckled. "What? He should just stand still so we can kill him?"

"Very funny."

To the left the opening was wider than most of the others and it appeared to be a large arena with reviewing stands arrayed on the sides.

"Huh!" Bennett grunted. "They've got their own coliseum."

Below and to the right, I spotted him. I raised the weapon and fired a shot off just before he ducked into yet another passage.

"I think I got a piece of him that time."

Bennett ran ahead of me down the stairs and looked at some spots on the floor. "Looks like it. Seems he's wounded."

Bennett glanced along the small dim corridor. "At least we now have some sort of trail to follow." He took a few steps before turning around. "I don't know if we should follow him down here unless we have a flashlight or something."

Behind us, a sound brought us around and we saw him scurrying back up the stairs.

"Damn!" Bennett shook his head. "Are there a lot of secret passages around here or what?"

"Who cares!" I headed for the stairs. "At least we can follow the trail of blood now."

CHAPTER THIRTY

A lot of noise could be heard coming from a doorway to the left, apparently through which Klakmonidos had ducked. I waved back to Bennett and we approached the open doorway cautiously.

Cocking my ear toward the noise, I asked, "Is he dying in there or what?"

More crashing noises could be heard.

Bennett shrugged. "Could be. Regardless, he may be very dangerous now. I've heard that some animals get dangerous when they're wounded."

"I hope not." I winced. "This guy was dangerous enough to begin with."

The noise diminished for a moment but then picked up again in intensity.

"Okay, but I think we can rule out him being in his death throes." He grinned. "Unless this is one of those Hollywood death scenes where he's gonna milk it for the entire last reel."

"Oh, God, I hope not." I shook my head and gripped the weapon tighter. "Maybe I can help ease him through to the other side, huh?"

Standing next to the doorway, I pivoted while bringing the weapon to bear and saw into the room. It seemed to be some sort of scientific laboratory from all the tables filled with chemistry sets and counters with electronic equipment. About half of these were already overturned by the big guy – the source of the most of noise we had been hearing – and he was in the process of upending another one when he spotted me. I brought the weapon to bear on him and pushed the firing stud.

Nothing happened.

Well, at least on my end. On his end, Klakmonidos heaved the table in my direction and I ducked out of the way as it crashed into the doorframe and fell into the hallway bent double.

"Oh, shit!"

"What's the matter?" Bennett asked.

"This thing's outta juice." I banged my palm on the side of the weapon.

"What?" Bennett grinned. "You think it's jammed?"

"Not exactly but that's normally how you get things to work right, isn't it?"

He nodded. "At least back on Earth anyways."

Looking around, I pointed down the corridor. "We have no idea what's going on out there. For all we know our guys might be losing the battle. Get out there and find out what's happening."

"But what are you going to do about him?" Bennett nodded toward the noisy room.

"I'll just keep threatening him with this thing while he tosses stuff at me I suppose."

"And what if he calls your bluff?"

"Then I'll run like hell." I motioned to him. "Now scoot!"

While we were beginning our chase through the Citadel, Saint Augustine was chewing on a problem. More and more souls were being drawn toward the portal open to Earth.

(Although I never got the chance to ask him what he was thinking, I got the story of his actions from others and I thought I could piece together sort of what his train of thoughts might have been.)

If many more of the souls were drawn away from the fight – that is, powering the weapon – I might not be able to defeat Klakmonidos, Satan. And if we lose in this instance, it could spell doom for all the souls recently liberated as well as the future of so many other souls.

Aside from merely hanging around the Citadel to lend their energies to the weapon I was planning on using against the big guy, Augie also had the freed souls "thinking happy thoughts" toward the demons.

I cannot say for certain whether any of this new born era of good feelings for the demons had any effect on the flow of the battle, it does seem to me that it did. There were times when demons got the drop on us and then paused, losing the advantage while our guys were able to overcome them.

Certainly there are times in battle when such incidents occur and people can simply write it off as luck or a sort of prescient nature that many soldiers – those who survive many battles – seem to exhibit. But this string of lucky circumstances occurred so many times and to so many people that I have wondered since if what Augie had said about the power of adoration might not be correct.

Regardless of that little metaphysical aside (none of which actually occurred to me at the time), Augie was worried about the number of souls getting drawn away from the scene of the battle and so he went to investigate and try to find some way to stop the large trickle before it became a flood.

What he found when he got there was a shocker: another source of evil seemed to be drawing the souls out of Hell back toward Earth and into another sort of captivity. He interposed himself between the deserters and the portal and did his "love flow" thing. Many of the flow seemed to wake from their trance and step aside.

These recruits then joined in his work, assisting him with stopping the mass exodus. Slowly by steadily, he was able to turn the tides around and shut off the current. Then, leaving a coterie of disciples there in the air above Anderson's HQ tent to keep the love flowing, he returned to the Citadel with the rescued souls.

He had Veronica and Elizabeth give a crash course to the souls in what was needed.

I wondered how these spirits could do both – participate in the greatest love fest since Woodstock *and* power the weapon.

Come to think of it, from Augie what had said, they were probably one and the same thing. And if I had ever doubted the power of love, that cured me.

Bennett had taken only a couple of turns along the passageways back toward the entrance when Grshluk ran into him. Literally. Bennett bounced back to his feet and helped the demon to his.

"Sorry, Grshluk, gotta run."

The demon grabbed his arm. "Wait, Bennett! I am happy to see you alive still. There has been some problem with the spirits… they were leaving…"

"Yeah, tell me about it. The weapon died!"

Nodding vigorously, Grshluk continued, "Yes, I know, but the one spirit has reversed the damage and the power should be restored by now. I was so worried that the short delay might have been…"

"Wait! You mean it's okay now?"

Grshluk nodded. "Yes, that's what I was…"

Bennett turned and ran back toward me, shouting, "Eric! Fire at will! FIRE AT WILL!!!"

CHAPTER THIRTY-ONE

The noise from the laboratory had decreased quite a bit and I think the big guy was catching on to our little problem. The last time I peered into the room, he waited several seconds before launching a table at me. It was plenty of time for me to fire the weapon but I didn't… well, because I couldn't.

Now it seemed the noises in the room, though diminished, were coming closer.

Wiping my sweaty palms on my trousers, I gripped the weapon and prepared to run for it. Footsteps drew closer and I saw the large shadow coming out of the room. It stopped at a distance noise.

It was Bennett, running, and shouting, "Fire at will!"

"About time!" I aimed into the room and depressed the firing stud. The beam sputtered at first then evened-out quickly. Stepping sideways, I turned the beam further into the room as the large shadow disappeared.

Tables flew through the air while I stood my ground in the doorway, firing into the room, trying to follow his frantic movements. The beam flung the tables back into the walls left and right.

By the time Bennett arrived, I was well into the room, following after Klakmonidos, who had retreated into the next room farther.

"Where is he?"

I stopped firing a moment. "The next room." More crashing could be heard. "Sounds like it's another room just like this one."

Looking around at the remnants surrounding us, Bennett shook his head. "I really don't think his successor is going to get much good out of this stuff."

Chuckling, I said, "After we're finished, I don't think anyone's going to even want the job."

"Okay, but let's finish it, okay?"

"Come on!"

In the next room, Klakmonidos was tearing the place up as we suspected.

As I trained the weapon, Bennett said, "He seems to be looking for something."

"Well, maybe we can help."

Klakky had stopped motion a moment and I opened fire. He ducked under the blast and it put a hole in the wall.

"You missed!" Bennett pointed.

"I know! I know!"

Klakmonidos ducked through the hole into the room beyond. I got off another shot just a split second too late. It went harmlessly through the hole where the big guy had been a moment before.

"Come on, Klakky. Keep still a minute." We started forward, Bennett holding out a hand.

"You want me to try?"

"I got it! I got it!" We reached the hole and saw a hole blasted in the farther wall of this smaller room. Klakmonidos was missing but could be heard further along.

"Damn! How long does this building keep on going?"

Bennett shrugged. "I don't know but I hope he doesn't get outside. It'll be impossible to get him out there."

"So, let's end it while we're still in here."

We followed Klakmonidos into the next section. A few small cubbies stood arranged around the sides of the room but there was no other door or window visible. This looked like the end of the road, one way or the other.

"This is it," Bennett whispered, "he's got nowhere else to go. Make it good, Eric."

"You got it!"

Bennett added nervously, "And don't punch any holes in the wall or he'll escape outside."

"Sheesh!" I rolled my eyes at him.

Klakmonidos was in the far corner of the room. He roared, raised his arms and shook his fists at us.

Once again, I raised the weapon at the monster. He grabbed at a metal pole just as I depressed the firing button.

Bennett saw Klakky's movement and ducked. "Watch out!

Ignoring both friend and foe, I kept my sights on the big guy and held firm to the weapon as it kicked out its beam. Klakmonidos' arms went upward in a roar as the beam connected.

A large explosion shook the building. I let up on the firing mechanism and squinted to see past the spots caused by the bright flash. When the light and dust cleared, we could see a hole in the wall leading to the outdoors. In the distance could be seen the steps leading up to Purgatory.

We approached the opening cautiously.

The visibility was pretty good in all directions and there was no cover between the Citadel and Purgatory, and the forest that lay a hundred yards beyond that.

"I don't see any sign of him." Bennett turned, grinning ear-to-ear. "Damn! I think you got him!"

Relaxing my hold on the weapon, which suddenly seemed to weigh a half-a-ton or so, I shook my head in disbelief. "Are you sure?"

Bennett stepped through the opening and looked around, hands on hips. Then he laughed. "Yep, no sign of him. You got him!"

Fatigue hit me and I was too tired to feel celebratory. All I could manage was an exhausted, "Finally!"

Before I could completely relax, there was a noise from behind. Bennett ducked again as I whirled, raising the elephantine weapon yet again.

Fortunately, it was just our pal Grshluk with Captain Anderson and a squad of American troops.

The Captain looked around. "Okay, where is the bastard?"

Stepping from behind me, Bennett answered, "He's gone, sir." He clapped a hand on my shoulder. "Eric blasted him to smithereens, sir!"

"That right, soldier?"

My weak nod was accompanied by an even weaker, "Yes, sir."

The troops set up a cheer and rushed forward. I was lifted to their shoulders as Bennett removed the BFG from my hands. It was good they carried me back to the main platform as I don't think I could have managed it on my own power.

Grshluk was filling in Bennett on the activity while we had been on our merry little chase. I was a bit hazy on all the details but I did get the fact that the demon forces had all been overwhelmed and were being held captive somewhere in the Citadel.

I won't say that I passed out, exactly, but I was in and out of things for a while there.

But the fun was not entirely over just yet.

CHAPTER THIRTY-ONE

Once we arrived at the main platform overlooking the Causeway, I was set back on my feet again as the soldiers arranged themselves again. The General was coming up the stairway. Behind him I could see some of the enemy combatants being led toward us, hands on their heads.

Captain Anderson took the initiative to go down and meet Old Ironguts halfway. He stopped and saluted smartly.

"Sir, the enemy commander has been dispatched and the threat removed."

Ironguts glanced up the steps and a hint of a smile played at the corner of his mouth. "Very good, Captain. Major Hopkins has brought me up to date on the situation here." He glanced around, spotted Grshluk and looked like he had swallowed something distasteful. "I understand we were assisted in our objective by, apparently, some lobster non-combatants."

"Yes, sir. Troopers Patterson and Wainwright made the initial contact and coordinated our actions with the friendlies."

The General glared at the Captain and seemed to fight back a sneer. "Very good." He looked up at us again. "And where are the men who neutralized the enemy leader?"

Anderson turned and motioned for me and Bennett to get down there. We rushed down the stairs and saluted the General as well.

"These are the men, sir. Troopers Patterson and Wainwright of Lieutenant Ordway's unit."

"Major Hopkins tells me you two were instrumental in creating a liaison with the underground element among the demon population. That was quick thinking, soldier, and... What the devil are these women doing here in a combat zone?"

Augie and the two ladies had appeared beside the Captain.

"Sir, we could not have done it without the help of these three. Elizabeth Larkspur, Veronica Symington, and Saint Augustine."

"Captain, what are these women doing in the combat zone?"

Before the Captain could answer, I responded, "These are spirits, sir. They and Saint Augustine here escaped from Purgatory."

The General was gritting his teeth. "I don't quite understand."

"They were…" I began but was interrupted.

"Excuse me, Eric," Augie said, "but we have to be going."

"Going?" I looked around. "Going where?"

The old fellow smiled broadly. "I am going to lead these souls away to heaven… if I can find the way." He glanced upward. "There are so many, and they are getting anxious. Not knowing how long it will take us, we had better get going."

"Oh, okay. Goodbye, I guess. And good luck!"

Elizabeth and Veronica waved their goodbyes and the three floated upward to rejoin the cloud of spirits floating above our heads. After a moment, the cloud rapidly diminished and vanished from existence.

The General was chewing the inside of his cheek. "Soldier, is there any way you can describe to me what just happened? Without going all religious on me?"

In spite of the little voice telling me not to, I grinned. "No, sir, I don't think I can."

"Very well, then." He glared at the Captain again. "Captain, I'd like to see the full report when this is all over. I'll expect it within the hour."

The Captain saluted. "Yes, sir."

"Well done, men." He turned away from us and signaled to a pair of Lieutenants. "Let's secure this area and set up our headquarters here so we can transition these… uh, civilians… back to a normal life." He shook his head. "Whatever the hell that was like."

While the General barked orders, the Captain motioned for the few of us to move out, back toward the portal. Bennett and I dragged along at the rear of the group, allowing them to pull further away with every step, as I had no desire to race. I still required some time to process exactly what went on.

At the sound of rapidly approaching bare feet, I glanced over my shoulder to see Grshluk catching up to us. We stopped and turned to him.

"Grshluk," I said, "I thought you'd be in the thick of getting the new government set up now that old Klakky is gone. With what you've done today, I'm sure you'll get a cushy job on the ruling council or whatever."

He laughed. "Not me! I have no interest in governance. Leave that to those so minded. I'm a librarian."

Bennett laughed. "It might be time for a change, you know. Stretch yourself. You're probably missing out on a good chance to be the one giving the orders."

"Yes, but it is still not within my character." Grshluk was true about that. "So, what happened at the end? Back in the laboratory?"

Bennett grinned. "Well, we blasted Klakmonidos back to his constituent subatomic parts." He looked at me, nodding. "Yes, when the dust cleared, there was nothing left of the old boy."

"I mean, are you sure he is gone?"

"Of course!" Bennett clapped me on the shoulder. "Eric blasted him out of existence."

Still looking worried, Grshluk looked at me somberly. "Eric, my friend. You have not said anything."

Glancing quickly at Bennett, I cleared my throat. "Well, to tell you the truth, it seemed like he was waiting for me to blast him. I think he could have outrun us anytime he wanted but he just kept banging around in each room making as much noise as possible. Like he was toying with us or leading us on." I shook my head. "At the end, he didn't try to dodge or escape , he just stood there holding onto a pipe or something."

"Yeah," Bennett nodded in agreement. "I thought he was going to use it against us."

Grshluk looked even more worried. "And what did he do with this 'pipe'?"

Bennett looked from me back to Grshluk.

I shrugged. "He was just holding it but when I pulled the trigger…"

"Yes?"

"I don't know, Grshluk. I thought he was going to duck or something, but he just stood there."

After a bit of a pause, Bennett nudged me. "And?"

I was re-playing the moment in my mind, trying to sort out anything odd. I mean, heck, the whole thing was odd, if you know what I mean but there was something that just didn't seem right about it even at the time. "It seemed like he pulled the pipe up when I blasted him. I remember thinking that maybe a bomb was going to go off or something but nothing happened."

Grshluk was intent. "A pipe? Could it have been a lever?"

I nodded. "Yeah, it was something like a lever… it didn't pull straight up…"

"What kind of lever?" Bennett looked from Grshluk back to me. "What do you know, Grshluk?"

"I don't know!" He flung his hands up and back down again. "He had so many demons working in the laboratories on so many different things." He shook his head. "None of the people in our group could ever find out exactly what he was doing but things like the weapon you used…" He shrugged. "Well, the word gets out."

"What could it have been?" Bennett took the demon's arm. "Have you heard anything about some secret weapon or something?"

"No, nothing like that." Grshluk shook his head. "But there was one thing…"

Bennett glanced at me, worried. "One thing?"

"Yes, it was only mentioned as a back-up plan… an escape clause of sorts…"

"But this thing couldn't have been tested, could it?"

Grshluk looked so worried, I took him off the hook. "What does it matter, huh? The war is over, Klakky's gone and things can get back to normal over here for Grshluk and his friends." I shrugged. "And if the big guy is in some parallel dimension… Hopefully, we'll never know." I grinned and began moving down the Causeway again.

Still I kept going over the scene in my head over and over again. And something else struck me as strange as well. It could be nothing – or my imagination – but I thought I should mention it.

As we reached the end of the Causeway, I turned to Bennett. "Did you happen to notice a strange glint in Irongut's eyes?"

The look Bennett gave me has haunted me ever since.

CHAPTER THIRTY-TWO

Well, that's the tale. Statistically speaking, it was a very successful operation. We only had the one casualty – Lieutenant Ordway – and about thirty guys who were wounded in the fracas. On their side, they lost about a hundred of the smaller demons (the friendlies used as shields and such) and about two hundred of the bigger guys. So, all things considered, it was a successful op.

Army intelligence moved in first thing and sequestered all of Satan's labs and rounded up as many of the scientists as they could to study what the fellows had been working on. I'm certain some of the things will make it to the market as new improved popcorn makers or such and, of course, some new video games.

I left the service shortly after… most the guys did as well. I think Ferguson went back to help in the rebuilding efforts and Vaudelet is working there as some sort of diplomatic liaison, but I've lost track of most the guys in the unit.

Grshluk stayed on at the library but does moonlight as a tour guide through the tunnels below the city. Seems they've been pumped out and are being repaired. Yeah, his sideline won't last long as they plan to get the subway running again.

Yes, Hell is now a prime tourist destination. I think the Papacy holds the concessional rights since the gateway is on their doorstep. The Pope has made a couple of his sermons from the Citadel and there are plans to build a cathedral there as well. Yes, the portal has been stabilized and enlarged. What a circus it has become!

Bennett has become an evangelical preacher, on television no less. I've heard his stuff but it seems a little too "out there" if you know what I mean; a little too apocalyptic for my taste. I've heard the "end time" talk since I was a kid and from what I've read, it has been going on for millennia. Every generation seems to think they are the last one. Seems like some sort of species-wide death wish or something, some feeling of inherent dissatisfaction with ourselves. It has been around forever and I don't expect that to change.

Military figures declined after the assault but wars and fighting did not stop. As someone had said, it could just be in Man's basic nature to fight over things, have greed and covetousness. No Satan required, I guess.

I've been on the talk circuit somewhat. That sort of thing gets old after a while, though, and I haven't done much in the recent past. As much as Ironguts said the mission was to be kept "under wraps" it sure went public mighty fast after we got back.

And most of that was Ironguts own doing.

It seems the excursion into Hell changed a lot of people but it seems the one who changed most was Ironguts himself. Many of those who knew him from before say he is a very changed man. Of course, most of those are supporting his campaign. Others, more quiet voices, are amazed the man has become so politically oriented.

Regardless, I can see from the latest poll numbers that he looks like the one to beat in the coming election in November. The incumbent doesn't stand a chance and the third-party poster child is a vague memory already.

All this has got me ruminating on those last few moments in the struggle against Klakmonidos. The more I look back at it, the more that pipe *does* look like a lever. I wish I had stopped to check out what the machine was that it was connected to. For all I know, the blast carried it into the next century or something.

And that strange gleam in General Strittmeier's eyes…

Could it be that the Big Guy in one world was transported into the body of the General? I have wondered.

But then the General seemed a little strange about this operation from the beginning. One would almost think he had been demon-possessed before the assault into Hell. The very idea that the war to end all wars could actually exist.

My plans?

I'm getting everything finalized here and liquidated. I've heard about the colonizing effort to see if that Earth-like planet found a few years ago will actually sustain life. It may not, of course, but there are several others in the vicinity if that one doesn't work out. It may be a fool's errand but I just feel the sudden urge to get off this rock.

Why?

Really…?!

I for one don't care to be here if Satan's going to be in the White House.

www.ingramcontent.com/pod-product-compliance
Lightning Source LLC
LaVergne TN
LVHW010604160826
845677LV00013B/3240

* 9 7 9 8 7 1 1 2 4 3 5 9 5 *